Also by Joan Lowery Nixon:

Joan Lowery Nixon

SPIRIT SEEKER

Delacorte  Press

Published by
Delacorte Press
Bantam Doubleday Dell Publishing Group, Inc.
1540 Broadway
New York, New York 10036

Library of Congress Cataloging-in-Publication Data
Nixon, Joan Lowery.
Spirit seeker / by Joan Lowery Nixon.
p.   cm.
Summary: To prove that her friend did not kill his parents, Holly
enlists the help of a clairvoyant.
ISBN 0-385-32062-0
[1. Extrasensory perception—Fiction.   2. Mystery and detective
stories.]   I. Title.
PZ7.N65Spi   1995
[Fic]—dc20   95-7090
                                                       CIP
                                                        AC

The text of this book is set in 12-point Goudy.

Book design by Julie E. Baker

Manufactured in the United States of America

September 1995

10 9 8 7 6 5 4 3 2 1

For Carol Farley
with love

Chapter One

Saturday. 2:00 A.M. Through the silence of the house came the creaking of the front door, the thud of dead bolts slapping into place, and the padding of muffled footsteps toward the kitchen. I had been lying in bed, waiting for him. With only a cold hollow where my stomach ought to be, I slid out of bed, threw a robe over my T-shirt, and ran barefoot down the stairs to confront my father.

Even though I was furious, I was frightened too. Don't get me wrong. I wasn't afraid of my father. I was scared of what he was doing to Mom . . . and to me.

I paused in the kitchen doorway and watched Dad pour a glass of milk. In the yellow light from the open refrigerator door, he looked awful. In spite of the fact that he's a tall, good-looking man, tonight his broad shoulders slumped inside a wrinkled, sweat-stained shirt, and his tie hung askew.

The lines in his face sagged with exhaustion, and smudged circles darkened his eyes.

"Dad, where were you?" I demanded.

He gave a start, sloshing the milk, which splatted against the faded linoleum floor; and as I flipped on the light switch, he squinted against the sudden brightness. "Oh, Holly," he said. "It's you."

Who else would it be? Not Mom. She'd be awake, I knew, lying curled in a ball, the blanket and sheet pulled almost over her head; but the last thing she'd do would be to come downstairs and confront Dad. Even when he went upstairs, Mom would pretend to be asleep.

Dad wearily unbuckled his shoulder holster and laid the holster and gun on the table. "Sit down, Holly," he said. "I need to talk to you."

I didn't want to hear what he had to say. *I* had something to say first. "Dad," I blurted out before I could change my mind, "you stood Mom up again. And she bought a new dress and got her hair done. What happened? Why didn't you call her?"

For an instant he looked bewildered. "Call her? I was on a case," he said.

"You just got *off* a case. You were supposed to be home for two days and take Mom out tonight to celebrate your anniversary."

Dad squeezed his eyes shut and rubbed his hands over the tight wrinkles that squiggled across his forehead. Mumbling against his palms, he said something that sounded like "Anniversary? Yeah, tonight."

"*Last* night," I said. "It's already morning." My

anger returned in a hot wave that bubbled up in my throat. Mom wasn't the only one Dad had stood up. I knew the feeling well. My class play— sure, it was a small part, but Dad had promised to be there—and my sixteenth birthday. Dinner at the elegant Charlie's 517 and tickets for a Broadway road show afterward at Jones Hall. The *three* of us. Only, as usual, it turned out to be just Mom and me.

Forget all that, I told myself. *Right now, this isn't about you. It's about Mom and Dad and what might happen to them.*

"You made Mom cry again. How could you not come home?" I asked him. I could have stopped there, but I didn't. Anger kept me going. "For a long time Mom stood at the window, watching the street, hoping you'd get home on time. I knew she'd given up when she called the restaurant and canceled the reservation. She went up to your room, shut the door, and cried. I could hear her." Defensively, I quickly added, "It wasn't disappointment about not going out to dinner. It was hopelessness because you didn't care enough to show up."

I stopped abruptly, not wanting to tell him I had also heard Mom's explosive fury and the words "I've had it. What's left but divorce?"

Dad just sighed and answered, "Your mother understands what a homicide detective's workload is like, Holly. You're sixteen. You're old enough to understand too."

"Well, I don't, and I think she's getting tired of having to be so understanding," I said. "There's a

3

whole staff of detectives in your department. Do they all get so involved in solving a case that they hardly come home at all? I don't think so." I reached for the word Mom had used. "You get obsessed with what you're doing. That's what the problem is."

Dad's jaw jutted stubbornly in a look I knew well. "You don't know what you're talking about. After a murder's committed, time runs out fast. We're talking about two—maybe three—days to look for clues and track down witnesses before the trail turns stale. And on top of everything else, we've got to try to keep curious neighbors, relatives, and the media from crowding around and accidentally destroying vital signs. Finding time to call home is often impossible. You know all this. Don't make me explain it again."

"Just a short call would keep Mom from feeling abandoned and from worrying," I persisted. This had happened so many times, ever since I was old enough to be hugged by Mom and smothered by the chill of fear that crept from her as we waited for Dad to return home—hours and hours late because he'd been working on a case.

I'd heard Mom beg Dad more than once, "Listen to me, Jake. Please, Jake. Why don't we move to a small town where there isn't as much crime as there is in Houston?"

But Dad had shaken his head. "No, Lynn. No small towns. You knew what my job was like when you married me. I've worked hard, and I'm respected here. Do you want to downgrade me to riding a desk or writing traffic tickets?"

4

Dad's voice broke into my thoughts. "Are you through with the recriminations, Holly? Because there's something important I need to tell you."

"You already told me," I muttered, "about how you have to work on cases, and you don't have time to call, and—"

Dad reached out and gripped my shoulders, practically pushing me into the nearest kitchen chair. I was so startled, my mouth and eyes flew open.

"Pay attention," he said as he settled facing me. "You're making this difficult. I have to ask . . . I need to know. . . . That boy you brought over here—Cody Garnett—"

Still defensive, I interrupted him. "I didn't just bring him over here, and he isn't 'that boy.' Cody and I have been friends since junior high. And now we've started dating."

Before Dad could answer, I went on. "You don't even know most of my friends. You didn't pay attention to Cody until he came to take me out on a date. You made it plain that night that you didn't like Cody much, even though you don't know him. He's really a neat guy. He was just shy about meeting you, and that's why he couldn't seem to find anything to say. But he's got a great sense of humor, and Mom likes him, and—"

Dad shook his head impatiently. "We're not talking about what I think of Cody. I want you to answer some questions for me. Have you met his parents?"

"Of course."

"How well do you know them?"

I shrugged. "They're just parents. Okay? They seem like nice people."

Dad frowned. "Holly, did you have a date with Cody tonight?"

"Why are you asking about Cody? What does Cody have to do with anything?"

"Just answer me, please."

"No, we didn't have a date."

The slight hiss of air through Dad's teeth was like a sigh of relief. "Do you know where he is?"

"He said something about having to go to his family's lake house."

"Which is . . . ?"

"Lake Conroe."

"For what reason?"

"There were some clothes he left there last month, like his new sports coat. His mom wanted him to wear it to some big thing they're all going to on Sunday and was upset that he'd forgotten to bring it home, so Cody decided to drive back to the lake house and get all his stuff."

"He has his own car?"

"Yes."

"Was he planning to spend the night at Lake Conroe?"

"I think so."

"Do you have any knowledge of when Cody planned to get back to Houston?"

"No."

Dad pulled a notepad and pen out of his shirt pocket. "How about an address or phone number for this lake house?"

"I don't know. I . . . What are you doing?" I

complained. "I feel like you're interrogating a suspect, and I'm the suspect."

"I'm sorry," he said. "These are questions that need answers, and I'm hoping you can help supply them."

"What for? You haven't told me why you're asking about Cody. What's going on?"

Dad waited a full minute, his eyes searching mine, before he spoke, but his voice softened as he said, "Holly, it's bad news."

The look in his eyes scared me, and it was hard to breathe. I whispered, "What kind of bad news?"

"I'd better start from the beginning, so you'll get the whole picture," Dad answered, his words dragging with a painful reluctance. "The police were called to a house where music was playing so loudly it disturbed a neighbor. The neighbor tried telephoning the occupants of the house, and when no one answered, he went to the house and peered through a living room window. He could see the man and wife lying facedown on the floor. He could see . . . blood, so he called the police."

"They were murdered?" I shivered, shoving away the horrible image, terrified at what Dad would say next.

Dad looked at me and grimaced as if he were in pain. "Yes. The people who were murdered were Cody's parents."

Words battered themselves against the blackness in my mind and wouldn't take shape. "Cody? . . . Cody? What happened to Cody?"

Dad stretched out one big hand, clumsily patting my shoulder as if he didn't know what else to

7

do. "Cody wasn't there, Holly," he said. "Two cars were in the three-car garage, both of them registered to his parents. There was no sign of Cody or his car."

Chapter Two

I woke up Mom, and she held me tightly, rocking back and forth on the edge of the bed, murmuring against my hair. When Dad came in, she pulled him down beside her and said, "Oh, Jake, how terrible! Cody's parents! Oh, Jake!"

Mom seemed to forget she was angry at Dad, and for a few minutes I could imagine that Mom and Dad loved each other just as much as they had when the house was warm and snug with the feelings that come with being a close, united family.

"We have to find Cody," I mumbled.

"We will," Dad said. "I contacted the police in Conroe. They had an address for the Garnetts' lake house."

I could picture uniformed cops knocking at Cody's door, waking him in the darkness with the news about his parents. Strangers telling him. People who wouldn't care.

9

I sat upright, twisting to face Dad. "Could we drive to Conroe? Could we break the news to Cody?"

"He's probably already been told," Dad said, and I groaned.

Mom gave my shoulders a squeeze, but she glanced at Dad as if she was disappointed in him. "We should have been there," she said. "He's Holly's friend, Jake. He's just a boy."

Dad's jaw stiffened. "Neither of you understand. It's important that Cody be . . . uh . . . located as soon as possible."

"But strangers . . . ," Mom began.

I interrupted, a chill like an icy hand shivering up my backbone. "Located?" I asked. "Are you saying that Cody is a suspect?"

Dad's uncomfortable silence was the only answer.

"Dad!" I shouted at him. "Cody's parents were murdered! It's going to be horrible for him when he finds out. You can't think of Cody as a suspect!"

Dad stared at the floor, but he said, "We have to explore every possibility."

"Don't do that!"

He looked up at me, surprised. "Don't do what?"

"Don't sound like you're reciting from a police manual. This is Cody we're talking about."

I realized that Mom had pulled her arm away from Dad's shoulders and was leaning against me as though the two of us had joined forces against him. "Holly's right," Mom said. "Cody's her friend."

Dad heaved himself to his feet. "Cody will get every consideration," he said. "No one's going to accuse him of anything. As of now, we have very little to go on."

"I can't believe you're saying these things about showing him consideration, then turning around and accusing him."

Dad's chin stiffened again. "In most multiple homicides which involve families, especially when there's no sign of forced entry, the lone survivor is the most logical suspect. You know about the Weinstrath murders, the Coul—"

I jumped to my feet, facing Dad. "This is not about old convictions! This is about Cody!" I yelled.

The bedside phone rang, and Dad swooped up the receiver, pressing it close to his ear. "Campbell here," he mumbled.

Holding my breath, I waited, wishing I could overhear what was being said.

"Okay," Dad said. "Thanks. I'll get back with you as soon as possible."

Slowly he replaced the receiver and looked up at me, his eyes darker and deeper than I'd ever seen them. "That was Conroe PD," he said. His voice was husky, and he cleared his throat a couple of times before he could continue. "Cody was not at his parents' lake house when the officers arrived, and, according to their report, there was nothing to indicate he'd been there recently."

Frantically I tried to think of a reason, but thoughts skittered in and out of my head like jagged stabs of light, disappearing before they began to make sense. "Maybe the police went to the wrong house. I've been to their lake house, and it's hard to find. I mean there are roads that wind around the lake and then dead-end into other roads, and besides, what if Cody slept outside on the porch or took out the boat?"

Mom squeezed my hand and said, "Calm down, Holly. There's no reason to panic."

But Dad had picked up the phone again and told whoever was on the other end, "Put out an APB. Cody Garnett. Brown hair, slender." He glanced at me. "How tall would you say Cody is, Holly?"

"Dad, you can't do this!" I exploded. "You're acting like Cody's a murderer!"

"I know how hard this is for you, Holly," Dad began.

"How could you know? You're determined that Cody's to blame without even finding out what really happened!"

"Holly . . ."

"Aren't people supposed to be considered innocent until they're proven guilty? Isn't that the way it works? So why are you sending out a bulletin to pick up Cody?"

"For his own good." Dad sighed. "I'm not going to try to explain while you're in this mood." His voice hardened as he asked, "How tall is Cody? Five-eleven? Six feet?"

"You're not being fair!" I shouted and ran into

my room. Fair? Not being fair? The word brought up a hateful memory, one that still taunted me, even condemned me. The memory rushed into my mind. I remembered so clearly when I was in the sixth grade. Three of us had stayed in the class-room during recess. We'd been allowed the special privilege of coloring in the banners we were mak-ing for the school's book fair.

One of the girls was Paula, who was so shy she spoke in gaspy whispers and turned pink every time Ms. Donavan, our teacher, called on her. The other was my best friend, Mindy. At least she said she was my best friend. She sat next to me at lunch, and walked home with me from school, and sometimes invited me to her house. It was special to be Mindy's best friend—particularly for me, un-used to the popularity that radiated in a wide swath around Mindy. Along with Mindy I was in-vited to everyone's birthday party. Kids I hardly knew talked and joked with me, and a boy named Robert even asked me for a date. Mom and Dad said no, I was much too young to date, but I didn't mind. I'd been asked, hadn't I? It was a heady feeling, and I loved every minute of being Mindy's best and special friend.

But on that day, the day Paula, Mindy, and I were supposed to be working on the banners, Mindy got bored and began to act silly. She started fooling around with the stuff on Ms. Donavan's desk, saying so many funny things I couldn't stop laughing. The more I laughed, the sillier she got.

Then Mindy picked up the ceramic statue of a

little girl reading and began waving it around. Paula, always cautious, said quietly, "I don't think you should do that. That's expensive. That's a Lladro."

I heard Paula and got nervous and stopped laughing, but Mindy didn't. Mindy giggled and stared at Paula with hostility. "What's a Lladro?" she said. "This looks like a silly old statue to me." She tossed it a few inches into the air and caught it.

Paula gasped. I did too.

"Mindy," I warned, "that's one of Ms. Donavan's favorite things. Her mother gave it to her years ago when she became a teacher. She said so."

"Are you taking Paula's side, Holly? I thought we were best friends." Mindy glared at me with a look that made me cringe. I sank back in my seat.

But Paula walked to the desk as Mindy tossed the statue and caught it again. "Don't do that," she ordered.

I'd never heard Mindy challenged by anyone, and I sucked in my breath.

Mindy glared at Paula. "Okay," she said. "If you're so crazy about this stupid statue, you take it." She tossed the statue to Paula.

Taken by surprise, Paula fumbled for it. But her fingers barely grazed the statue, and it dropped to the floor near her feet, smashing into a dozen pieces.

Neither Paula nor I could move. We just stared, openmouthed.

The door to the classroom opened. Somehow, Mindy was in her seat as Ms. Donavan entered the room.

"Oh, Paula!" Ms. Donavan cried. "How could you?"

She bent to pick up the pieces, and as she rose, her eyes were damp.

"I'm sorry," Paula murmured, and tears rolled down her face too. "It was an accident."

The accident wasn't Paula's fault, and I knew it wasn't fair for her to take the blame. My lips parted as I tried to get the courage to speak the truth, but Mindy slowly turned in her seat, her gaze penetrating mine. I wanted to tell what had happened. I desperately wanted to. But I realized that if I did, I'd lose Mindy as a friend, and I'd lose the other friends I'd made because of Mindy. I was scared that nobody would like me.

"What's done is done," Ms. Donavan said, her eyes still on the broken statue. "Run outside, girls. You've got about ten more minutes of recess. We'll work on the banners later." She stooped to pick up the pieces.

Outside in the hallway, I felt sick to my stomach. "Paula," I managed to say, but Mindy grabbed my hand and pulled me toward the playground.

"She dropped it. You saw her," Mindy said.

Paula looked at me, but she didn't say a word. Neither did I, not then and not later.

A few weeks later, Paula was no longer in our school. Ms. Donavan told us that Paula's father had been transferred to another state. She'd left

Houston, but the memory of what I'd done—what I *hadn't* done—stayed with me. It taunted me through Mindy's eyes, and I no longer wanted to be her best friend. I knew the difference between right and wrong. I should have stood by the truth and stood up for Paula. I shouldn't have allowed her to take the blame.

There was nothing I could do to make amends to Paula, and if the incident still bothered her, I'd never know. But I did know that I had another chance to do the right thing. I could stand up for Cody, if he were innocent.

But of course Cody was innocent.

I heard Dad calling for me to come back, so I hurried to their bedroom, where Dad was talking on the phone, repeating his guess to whoever was on the other end of the line.

He looked in my direction. "Holly? Holly, pay attention. Am I remembering correctly that Cody drives an old, slightly beat-up blue two-door Thunderbird? Is that description right?" Dad asked. I refused to answer him. I hated Dad's good memory. Even when I went out on a date, he was more a detective than a father.

Dad turned his back on me, but I heard him say, "Look up the registrations under Sam and Nelda Garnett. You should be able to get the information. The cars in the garage were a Cadillac, two—maybe three years old—and a fairly new BMW."

When Dad hung up, he turned to face me. His shoulders drooped, and his eyelids sagged at the outer corners like crooked window shades. "I'm trying to help Cody," he told me.

"You're not!"

"If I do my job right, I will."

Mom put an arm around my shoulders and said, "It's nearly four o'clock. Since it's Saturday, we can sleep in, so let's get back to bed. We'll all think better when we're rested."

I wanted to snap at her for using her teacher voice. "Don't talk to me like I'm one of the kids in your fourth-grade class!" But my quarrel wasn't with Mom. It was with Dad, and Mom did have a point. I needed time to think, to work out some kind of plan to help Cody. He'd need someone, and I wouldn't let him down.

As I got to my feet, a sudden thought struck me so hard that I gasped. "Dad!" I said. "What if Cody didn't get to the lake house because . . . because he was at home when his parents were murdered, and whoever did it kidnapped Cody and used his car? What if . . . ?" I couldn't finish.

Dad's forehead crinkled, and I realized he'd been aware of this possibility all along. "Forget it, Holly. Don't borrow trouble," he mumbled. "There were no signs of a struggle."

"But it could have happened. That's why you ordered an all points bulletin, wasn't it?"

"It had something to do with it."

My throat ached as I choked out the words "I'm sorry, Dad. I got so angry . . . I didn't mean the things I said."

"No matter," he answered and shifted uncomfortably. "We'd better do what your mother suggested, and go to bed."

I wished he'd reach out to me, but Dad has never been the kind of person to show how he feels.

I wandered back to my room and shut the door. A snapshot of Cody was propped against the lamp next to my bed, and as I picked it up, studying it intently, I could feel his arm around my shoulders, his breath against my cheek, his lips against mine. In this photo Cody was dressed in swim trunks and a faded T-shirt and was leaning against a surfboard propped in the sand. His smile was broad, and I'm sure that a moment after the picture had been taken, he'd burst out laughing.

"Oh, Cody!" I whispered, hurting for him. I gently put the photo back in place and flopped onto my bed. I knew I'd never be able to sleep. Was Cody dead too? Or was he alive somewhere, at the mercy of the person who had murdered his parents?

I struggled to my feet and began to pace as I attempted to make sense of all I'd heard. There'd been no forced entry, Dad had said. No sign of a struggle. That meant Cody couldn't possibly have been in the house when the murders took place. Cody was tall and strong. He would have put up a fight to try to save his parents. He never would have gone peacefully with the murderers, no matter what. Cody had told me he was going to the lake house, so that's what he did, didn't he?

I shook myself. Of course he did. What kind of

a friend was I if I allowed myself to doubt him for even a minute? Somehow, in some way I didn't understand right now, when the police had gone to the Garnetts' lake house, they'd missed him. Cody'd be able to tell us why. In the meantime, I'd do what Mom had said. I'd go to bed and try to sleep.

I visualized the Garnetts' trim two-story brick house with bright borders of pink and white begonias around the front and down the walkway, the lawn a thick, smooth carpet of St. Augustine grass. "Mom's the gardener," Cody had told me the first time I'd seen his house.

"It's neat," I'd said. "It looks like a painting."

But now there'd be yards of yellow police tape wound between the trees and over the lawn, a tangled web barring the doorway. If Cody, unaware of what had happened, were to return home, what would he think? What would he do? I couldn't let him walk into that house alone!

I abruptly stopped my pacing and grabbed a bedpost for support. I knew what I had to do, even as a voice in my head asked, *Go to Cody's house? A murder scene? In the middle of the night? Are you crazy?*

If I really believed that Cody was innocent—and I had to! I had to!—then I couldn't let this boy I cared about take the shock alone.

I scrambled through my closet, pulled on jeans and a T-shirt, and brushed my tangled hair. I reached for the wide silver and amber barrette Mom had given me on my last birthday. But as I picked it up from the top of the dresser, the smooth, usually cool amber suddenly felt so warm against my palm that I jumped at the touch. It seemed to glow with a red-gold heat.

Startled, I dropped the barrette on the dresser top, where it lay under the table lamp, reflecting the light. I realized it must have picked up the heat from the lamp, so I picked it up again, pulled back my hair, and fastened the barrette in place.

As silently as possible I opened my door and crept down the stairs. In the kitchen, using only the glaring green light from the clock on the microwave, I scribbled out a note telling Mom and Dad where I'd be, before I slipped out of the house through the back door, the keys to Mom's gray Camaro in hand. It was Saturday, so Mom wouldn't be going to school, and she wouldn't need her car—at least not for a few hours.

I drove almost a mile to West University, to the street on which Cody lives. I drew nearly opposite his house and parked the car, prepared to wait. Cody would be coming home—he *had* to be coming home—and I was going to be there for him when he arrived.

It was a hot, sticky September night, yet I was so frightened, my body was cold. I tried not to look at the house, but it loomed like a dark demon, demanding my attention. The police had left the drapes open, so the front windows gaped with blank, glassy eyes. The house was empty, yet, as I looked at it, it throbbed like a heartbeat.

Strange, shivery pinpricks of light appeared, then vanished.

Is someone already inside the house? Could it be Cody? I wondered.

I had to know.

Although I realized the wish was totally unreasonable—surely Cody would have reacted to the crime tape—I slipped out of Mom's car, quietly shut the door, and walked across the street, ducking under the crime scene tape. Close to the living room windows I could see the reason for the tiny flashes of light. The VCR on top of the television batted out a consistent *12:00, 12:00, 12:00,* a mindless robot waiting for someone to arrive and reset it.

I cut across the front lawn, ducking under the tape again, and circled toward the back of the house. If the door to the unattached garage was unlocked, at least I could find out whether Cody's car was there.

Moonlight was merely a pale shimmer, scarcely enough to light the way. But over the years I had visited Cody's house often, and I knew I could walk down the driveway to the back of the house, where it met the high board fence that enclosed the backyard, then follow the fence to the narrow door that opened into the garage.

Once past the brick, I reached out to steady my steps. My fingers touched the rough boards and slid across to the cold metal latch. To my amazement the latch suddenly moved, and I jumped back to keep from being struck as the gate whipped open.

A dark shape stepped through the opening, and a goggle-eyed face peered into mine. "Don't you know there was a murder here?" a voice whispered, and strong fingers gripped my shoulder.

I tried to scream, but my throat was so paralyzed with fear, all that came out was a choking gurgle.

Squinting behind thick glasses, the man leaned forward so that his nose was just inches from mine. "Are you here because of the murder?" he asked. "It's not a safe place to be. He might come back."

"W-Who might come back?" I stammered.

"The murderer."

I tried to take a step backward, but the man's grip increased. "Say, aren't you one of Cody's friends?" he asked, and his voice softened.

"Y-Yes," I said.

"I thought you looked familiar. Remember me? I live next door. I'm Ronald Arlington. Close friend of the family." Without a pause he asked, "Where's Cody?"

I shivered, wishing I knew. "He went to their lake house," I answered. I well remembered talkative Mr. Arlington. Cody and I had tried to avoid Mr. Arlington ever since the time he'd corralled us on the driveway to talk and wouldn't stop until Cody's mom had come outside, politely insisting that dinner was getting cold.

"Ronald is lonely," Mrs. Garnett had explained that evening as she served the salads. "He's retired and seems to have nothing to occupy his time. Recently his wife left him and threatened to file for divorce."

"He has time to butt into everybody's business," Mr. Garnett had said.

"Now, Sam," Mrs. Garnett had begun, but Mr. Garnett persisted.

"Yes, he does. He comes right out and asks what people paid for things—like a new sweater or a new car—and then he tells everyone. And he has to know who's doing what and why, and he's always got some kind of inside story about celebrities and politicians and stuff that he's supposed to know for a fact."

"I think he just wants a little attention," Mrs. Garnett had said.

"Or a drink," Mr. Garnett had said with a knowing wink.

"He's really not such a bad old guy," Cody had answered.

"Let's please talk about something else," Mrs. Garnett had begged.

I hadn't given Mr. Arlington another thought . . . not until he'd popped through the gate, scaring me almost to death.

"The police came into my house and talked to me," Mr. Arlington whispered into my face. "I told them I was the one who couldn't stand the loud music, so I came over and looked in the window when the Garnetts didn't answer their telephone." Nervously he glanced around, as though he might be overheard. "I'm the one who discovered the bodies," he said. "And I turned off the master switch to the house because the music was driving me crazy. The television people and the newspaper reporters came, but I didn't tell them that . . ." He broke off, fumbling with his words as though they were loose teeth, as he added, "Well, what I did tell them will be in the morning paper and the early newscasts."

He released my shoulder, but I didn't attempt to leave. Obviously Mr. Arlington had information I wanted.

"What didn't you tell them?" I asked.

He gave a quick turn to look over his shoulder. "Never mind," he said.

"If it's important, the police should know about it."

His eyes became slits. "They don't have to know everything."

Maybe he knew something, maybe he didn't. I wasn't sure how to reach him, so I said the first thing that came into my mind. "If it's something that will help them catch the murderer, then I know you'll tell them. Otherwise, you'd be helping the murderer."

"The murderer might come back," Mr. Arlington repeated in a husky whisper. "I live alone here, and I'm not so young anymore."

I wasn't getting anywhere, so I asked directly, "Did you tell the reporters that Cody wasn't home?"

He nodded. "They asked where he was, but unfortunately, I didn't know. I just told them what time I heard his car leave. He was driving down the driveway a little too fast, and when he does that, his car squeals, and I happened to look at the clock, and it was a good thing I did, I guess."

I took a deep breath and asked, "What time did Cody leave?"

"Twenty-seven minutes after seven," he said.

I had to ask. "And what time did the murders take place?"

"I asked the police that very thing, but they told me the medical examiner will determine that."

I tried to phrase my question another way. "What time was it when you heard the loud music?"

"Somewhere between nine and nine-thirty. This time I didn't look at the clock, so I can't be sure."

Joyfully I blurted out, "Then Cody couldn't have been at home!"

"That's what I already said."

A car suddenly pulled onto the driveway, its headlights spotlighting us.

Mr. Arlington squinted and ducked, throwing an arm up to protect his eyes.

The car door opened and slammed, and I heard the anger in Dad's voice as he demanded, "Holly, what do you think you're doing here?"

Chapter Three

The sky was beginning to lighten, pearly gray streaks from the east smearing the blackness. "I had to be here," I said. "When Cody comes home . . ."

"*If* Cody comes home . . ."

"*When.* It has to be *when.*" I could be as stubborn as my father. "Someone who cares about him should be here for him."

Dad winced, and I put a hand on his arm. "As a friend," I said. "Dad, you know Cody and I have been friends since junior high."

Mr. Arlington's head swiveled from me to Dad and back again, as if he were a spectator at a tennis match. "You remember me?" he asked Dad, his voice barely a whisper. "I'm the one who found the bodies and called the police. I told that other detective—Mr. Martinez—what I heard and saw."

"Yes, Mr. Arlington," Dad said. "We appreciate your help."

"It's going to be on the morning TV news."

Dad glanced at the open gate to the backyard, its torn yellow tape trailing on the driveway. "This is a crime scene, Mr. Arlington," he said. "It's off-limits."

"I didn't disturb anything." For a moment Mr. Arlington looked frightened. He suddenly held his watch close to his eyes and said, "I don't want to miss the early news, so if you don't need me . . ."

Without waiting for an answer, he scuttled across the driveway, toward the front door of his house.

In contrast to the Garnetts' large, beautiful home, Mr. Arlington's dark brick house was small, plain, and old. Back in the 1980s, when Houston was booming and lots of people had a great deal of money, West University boomed too. One by one the tiny brick homes and their lots were bought for hundreds of thousands of dollars, the houses were demolished, and expensive homes rose in their place. I guess builders expected the entire area to change, but suddenly the oil business cratered, buyers almost disappeared, and many West University blocks were left in a frozen pattern of mansions interspersed with modest bungalows.

The spreading morning light outlined a pickup truck coming down the block, rolled newspapers flying from its windows and slapping the sidewalk. Police cars began to arrive, some marked, some unmarked. Officers in uniform and plainclothes detectives climbed from their cars, some cradling coffee mugs as though they were lifelines. The detectives mumbled greetings to Dad, exchanged brief information, and entered the Garnetts' house and yard. For a moment my mind went with them into the scene of blood and gore. I shuddered, vividly aware that Dad had to go through this kind of horror over and over.

He turned sharply to look at me, and I realized I'd whimpered.

I wanted to hug Dad, to hold him tightly and pull him away from the horrible specter of violence and death. But, instead, I took a deep breath. "I'm okay," I lied.

A Channel 2 truck drove up, followed by one from Channel 13. Reporters and camera operators zoomed out like bees from a hive, and soon the sidewalk was covered with a tangle of cables and equipment.

A reporter, microphone in hand, propelled herself toward Dad.

"Go home, Holly," Dad ordered.

"I can't, Dad," I said and begged, as angry tears blurred my vision, "Please don't make me!"

Dad hates tears and doesn't know how to handle them. I heard Dad tell Mom once that whenever a suspect broke down and cried, it was hard for him to stay in the room. I know he thinks that Mom and I—so much alike with our red hair and green eyes—are a pair of emotional weaklings, but at that moment I didn't care.

"Please," I repeated.

Dad answered gruffly, "You can stay for a while, but don't get underfoot, and don't talk to the media."

Dad didn't need to worry. The people from the press and television stations, who continued to arrive, weren't the least bit interested in me. Zeroing in on Dad, they asked, "Are there any new developments? Have you arrested the Garnetts' son? Is he a suspect?"

I was shocked that Cody was guilty in their minds, simply because he'd survived and his parents hadn't.

A guy with a camera glanced at me and asked, "Are you anybody?"

I shook my head. I wasn't the kind of anybody he was looking for. He joined the group surrounding Dad.

Mr. Arlington poked his nose outside his door. He scuttled out to pick up his newspaper, then hurried back inside his house.

The temperature rose rapidly, heat spreading over us like melted butter in a swarmy yellow puddle, so I claimed a patch of deep shade under one of the large oak trees on Mr. Arlington's front lawn and sat cross-legged on the grass.

Curious neighbors drifted over to watch the action, lining the sidewalk across the street as though they were waiting for a parade to pass by. Two more cop cars arrived, and the officers joined Dad on the driveway, elbowing through the group of reporters. After briefly talking with Dad, one of the officers headed for the Garnetts' backyard. The others stayed on the lawn, talking to each other. What were they doing? Who or what were they waiting for?

Mr. Arlington came out of his house again and moved in a slow, sidewise gait to where I was sitting. "They showed me on TV, and my name was in the story in *The Houston Post*. I wish they had left me out of it." He shook his head sadly and wrapped his arms about his chest as though he was trying to protect himself. "I wish . . . I wish I hadn't told them anything," he said.

"You did the right thing," I reassured him.

He squatted down and tilted his head, peering at me from the corners of his eyes. "You said if I didn't tell them all I knew, I'd be helping the murderer."

I was sure of it! Mr. Arlington did know something that would help Cody! I tried to think carefully before I spoke. It was like approaching a skittish horse. One quick move, and off he'd run.

"If the police catch the murderer, he can't come back. But as long as they don't know who the murderer is, he's out there, and he can murder again."

Had I gone too far? I held my breath, waiting to see what Mr. Arlington would do next.

His eyeballs darted like swimming fish behind his thick glasses. He frowned in thought, then suddenly got to his feet and strode purposefully toward Dad.

I jumped up and followed.

"Detective Campbell," Mr. Arlington said, "no matter the consequences, I must explain to you

30

why I was in the Garnetts' backyard when you arrived this morning."

This caught a nearby reporter's attention. He hurried toward Dad, and other reporters, noticing his actions, quickly joined the group.

Mr. Arlington flinched and said to Dad, "Could we talk privately? Without the reporters?"

"Of course," Dad told him and began to lead the way toward Mr. Arlington's house.

But Mr. Arlington, struggling to keep up with Dad's stride, cried, "No! Not in the house! Oh no!"

Dad stopped, surprised, and Mr. Arlington, his face flushing a deep red, stammered, "I—I'm not a good housekeeper, and it—it's not very tidy. When my wife left me, she took most of the furniture, and . . . If you could just keep the reporters away, we could talk over there, under the tree."

Dad waved off a TV cameraman, ordered a reporter to keep her distance, and walked out of their hearing with Mr. Arlington. Naturally, I walked with them. I wasn't the press. I wasn't a threat. For the moment I was invisible.

Mr. Arlington gulped loudly, then said, "I wanted to look around the back of the house, in case the police missed something the murderer had left behind. And I wanted to see if there might be bloody fingerprints on the board fence behind the garage. You know, the fence that divides the Garnetts' yard from mine."

Dad stiffened. "What fingerprints are you talking about?"

Mr. Arlington held up his hands palms out and

waved them like two white flags. "Fingerprints that might have been left on the fence when the murderer climbed over and ran through my yard."

"You saw the murderer?"

"Yes . . . well, no. I mean, not exactly."

Dad bent his head toward Mr. Arlington's. "Tell me what you saw," he said.

Mr. Arlington nodded, gulped, and said, "It was so dark I wouldn't be able to identify him. But he was tall and a well-built, muscular type. He practically flew over the fence between my house and the Garnetts', then hoisted himself over my back fence."

"You're absolutely sure of this?"

Mr. Arlington gulped again and actually shivered, but he didn't change his story. "I told you, it was dark, and I couldn't make out details, but yes . . . I'm sure I saw someone go over that fence."

"When did you see him?"

"As I came around the side of my house, crossing the Garnetts' driveway on my way to knock at their front door."

"You could see all this from their driveway?"

"Yes. I could see somebody jump over both fences."

Dad walked with Mr. Arlington to the exact spot and, of course, I did too. Poor Mr. Arlington, who looked more frightened by the minute, was right. It *would* be possible to see someone climb over both fences.

That meant I was right! Cody *was* innocent. My heart pounded so loudly I could hear it in my ears.

"Why didn't you tell me about this sooner?" Dad asked.

"I should have, but I was afraid to," Mr. Arlington said. "I thought the murderer would come back." He shivered again as he added, "I still think so, and I'm still afraid, but I want to do what is right." He pointed at a chubby woman, wearing purple shorts and top, who was standing with a group of onlookers across the street. "There's Mrs. Rollins," he said. "She lives in the house behind mine. Maybe she heard or saw something."

He motioned frantically to Mrs. Rollins, calling her to join them. After a moment of surprise, Mrs. Rollins, and a shorter, younger carbon copy, dropped from the group like a couple of overripe grapes and came toward us.

Mr. Arlington repeated his story and said, "Did you hear anyone in your yard last night? Around nine or so?"

Mrs. Rollins's daughter poked the center of her chin with an index finger and said, "Was that when Tiger started barking, Mama?"

"That stupid dog's always barking," Mrs. Rollins said.

"But last night he was barking different. Remember? You even said a cat must have got in the yard."

Mrs. Rollins nodded. "I guess I did say that, Trudy, but I don't remember what time it was."

"Was your dog loose in the yard?" Dad asked.

"Yeah. Tiger's more of a house dog, but he's getting old and he needs to go out often. We leave him outside for a while before we go to bed."

Trudy grew so excited she bounced up and down on her toes. "So it wasn't a cat!" she cried out. "Think of that! It was the murderer!" She giggled. "I wonder if Tiger got a taste of him!"

"Tiger bites?"

"Not real bad bites, but he nips if he thinks someone's an intruder. He tore our plumber's pants leg, and when the cable TV man came, he—"

The reporters had edged closer and closer, and now their questions piled one on top of another in a confusing jumble, punctuated by Trudy's squeaks and Mr. Arlington's loud exclamations.

Dad didn't try to outshout them. He grabbed one of Mr. Arlington's arms and led him toward the backyard.

I started to follow them, but just then one of the neighbors across the street shouted, "There he is! There's Cody!"

He had parked down the street, as close as he could get to his house with the swarm of trucks and cars in the way, and he stood without moving, staring at his house as though what he saw weren't real but part of a bad dream. As he took in the police tape, he stumbled forward, his eyes frantically searching the crowd. "What's going on?" he cried out. "Where's my mom? Where's Dad?"

Giddy with relief, I shouted Cody's name and ran toward him, grabbing his shoulders. For a moment he didn't seem to see me or know me, but finally he focused in on my face long enough to question me. "Holly, where are my parents? What's happening here?"

Dad stepped up and took charge of the situation. "Please come with me, Cody," he said, and led Cody around to the side of the house, through the back gate, and into the kitchen. I wasn't about to get left out, so I followed.

"Sit down, please," Dad said gently.

Without question, Cody did, staring down at the tabletop as if he were mesmerized. I sat beside him and reached for his hand, holding it tightly. Dad pulled out a chair across from Cody and straddled it.

Briefly, without details, he quietly told Cody that his parents had been murdered.

"Cody," I whispered, "I'm sorry, I'm terribly sorry."

Cody wrenched his hand away from mine, dropped his head onto his arms, and sobbed loudly, the way a little kid would cry.

Dad squinted with embarrassment and got up from the table, standing at the sink where he could stare out the window into the backyard, but I put an arm around Cody's shoulders and held him tightly.

Finally Cody's sobs became shudders. He shoved back his chair, grabbed a wad of tissues from a box on the counter, and mopped at his face. His face was swollen, red, and blotchy. I wanted to comfort him, but I realized that no one could possibly know how horrible he must feel.

"How did it happen?" Cody asked.

"They were stabbed with a knife." Dad fixed his gaze on a wall rack that held a graduated set of knives with polished black-and-white bone handles. Cody and I followed Dad's glance. The third slot from the left was empty, leaving a gap like a lost tooth. "Incidentally," Dad said, "we haven't been able to find the missing knife."

Cody groaned and swayed. I hung on to him, trying to steady him. "When . . . when did it happen?" Cody asked. "And why? Do you know who did it?"

Dad sat down again and countered with a question of his own. "Are you up to supplying us with some information?"

Cody's voice grew stronger, even a little belligerent, as he snapped, "You didn't answer *my* questions." He still hadn't looked at me. He didn't even look at Dad but kept his gaze firmly on the tabletop.

I told myself that Cody was probably still in shock, yet there was something about the way he was behaving that made me uncomfortable. I believed in his innocence because he was my friend, and after what Mr. Arlington told us, I was positive Cody was innocent. But I had the creepy feeling that Cody was hiding something.

It wasn't Cody Dad spoke to, it was me. "You may leave now, Holly."

Cody surprised me by grasping my hand and inching his chair toward mine. "Please let her stay, Mr. Campbell," he said, and for an instant his voice wavered. "Right now I need a friend."

His hand was clammy, and fear trembled like an electric shock from his body into mine. "Don't be afraid," I told him. I willed him to look at me

36

so he could read the message in my eyes, but again he glanced down at the table.

"Let me stay, at least for a little while," I begged Dad.

Dad didn't give me a yes or a no. As though I'd become invisible, he went on to tell Cody everything he'd told Mom and me about the loud music and the complaining neighbor who'd discovered the crime. "That's all we know at this time," he said. "We haven't got the medical examiner's report yet or the results found by the crime lab." He paused. "Now, Cody, I'd like to ask you a few preliminary questions. Holly, you may be excused."

"What kind of questions?" Cody asked.

"Dad!" I complained. "Cody wasn't even here!"

"Holly!"

"Mr. Arlington told you he saw the murderer. At least he thought he saw a man jump the back fences. Instead of bothering Cody with a lot of questions, why don't you check out Mr. Arlington's story?"

"His story—such as it was—will be thoroughly investigated. We'll look into every angle of this case, which includes getting as much information as I can from Cody." He paused before he said again, "Holly, you may be excused."

Dad's tone of voice told me that I'd pushed him as far as he would go, so with a last squeeze to Cody's hand, I got up and opened the back door.

"Holly's right. I wasn't here when . . . when it happened," Cody said. "I left for our lake house around seven-thirty. Mom and Dad were getting ready for some big party they were going to. Everything was fine. No problems."

Dawdling as much as I could, I slowly closed the kitchen door, unfortunately shutting out the voices.

As I walked through the gate to the driveway, where the heat rose in dusty waves from the glaring pavement, I saw Dad's partner coming toward me. With him was a middle-aged woman dressed in a loose red T-shirt and white shorts. She wore large earrings and a chain around her neck. Both had that shimmery, expensive look of real gold.

Bill Carlin wasn't as tall as Dad, but he had the same stocky build. About ten years older than Dad, Detective Carlin was missing most of his hair, and his weather-beaten face was deeply creased around the eyes and mouth. He'd been married and divorced three times and liked to say that it was much easier being a bachelor than trying to explain to a wife why his job wasn't a nine-to-five.

He looked surprised when he saw me. "What are you doin' here, Holly?"

"Cody Garnett is a friend of mine."

"I was told that your dad's talkin' to him inside the house?"

I gestured toward the back door. "In the kitchen."

Carlin said to the woman, "If you don't mind waitin' a minute out in the yard, Mrs. Marsh, I'll get my partner."

They went inside the gate, and I stayed where I

was on the other side of the fence, hoping to over-hear whatever was going to take place.

Carlin went inside the house, and a few moments later the door opened and shut again and I heard him introducing the woman to Dad.

"Mrs. Marsh is a neighbor directly across the street," Carlin said. "She has somethin' to tell us about the time Cody left his house last night."

Mrs. Marsh hesitated, then said, "I don't see how it has any bearing on what happened. I mean, Cody had left the house before his parents . . . Oh, dear! I can't believe this could happen in our neighborhood."

"Please, Mrs. Marsh," Dad said quietly. "Did you see Cody leave his house?"

"Yes, both times."

I stiffened, not daring to breathe.

"*Both* times?"

"I was just coming back from taking my dog for a walk when Cody drove off the first time," Mrs. Marsh said. "It was a few minutes before seven-thirty, I know, because there was a television program on the Arts and Entertainment channel that started at seven-thirty, and I made sure I was home in time to see it."

As she stopped for breath, Dad stepped in. "Did you see Cody return?"

"No," she answered, "but awhile later I remembered I hadn't watered the hanging plant on my front porch, and with all this heat, well, I couldn't let it go another day, so I got my watering can and went outside."

"What time was this?"

"During the nine o'clock commercials. I'd switched to Channel 2."

"Did you see Cody at this time?"

"Yes, I did. Isn't that what I said?"

I could hear the tension rise in Dad's voice. He was sure—so sure the murderer had to be Cody. I leaned against the rough boards, feeling a little sick to my stomach, listening because I had to.

"What was he doing?"

"Getting into his car. While I was on the porch, he drove away."

"Where was it parked?"

"On the street."

"Not on the driveway?"

"No. On the street."

"Are you sure it was Cody you saw and not someone else?"

"I guess I ought to know Cody when I see him. Besides, there's a streetlight right there, so I could see him clearly. His car too. I'm familiar with Cody's car."

"Did the loud music coming from the Garnetts' house disturb you?"

Mrs. Marsh cocked her head like a sparrow as she thought. "Loud music. Yes, I heard the loud music. I hear it often. You know, with a teenage boy in the neighborhood . . . I mean, all the teenagers seem to be partially deaf when it comes to music and have to turn the volume way up and . . ."

"So you heard the music the second time Cody drove away."

"Wait. I didn't say that. I told you I heard the music, but was it when I saw Cody or was it later? I can't remember."

"Is there anything else you can tell us?"

Mrs. Marsh hesitated. "Uh . . . no. I didn't like the program on Channel 2, so I decided to read in bed. I didn't see the mur—uh, anyone else arrive at the Garnetts' house." Her voice brightened as she added, "I heard that Mr. Arlington saw the murderer run across his yard and into the Rollinses' yard! You know what that means, don't you?"

Before Dad could answer, she nodded knowingly and said, "I bet he was running toward his car, which was probably parked on the street behind us. It wasn't parked in or near the Garnetts' house, or I would have seen it. So it couldn't have been just a random burglary. Somebody deliberately planned to murder the Garnetts and—"

Carlin interrupted this time, saying, "Thank you, Mrs. Marsh. Here's my card. If you think of anythin' else we should know, please call this number."

Anything else? I groaned inside and watched Mrs. Marsh push through the gate and hurry across the street, where I knew she'd find an immediate audience in the other onlookers.

Suddenly I heard Cody's voice, high-pitched and nervous. "I heard what Mrs. Marsh told you, and it's not what you think."

"Are you denying that you left your house, returned, then left again?" Dad asked.

"I'm not denying it. I was halfway to Conroe when I remembered I'd forgotten the key to the lake house, so I came back for it."

"Why didn't you tell me that in the beginning?"

"Because of the way it looked. I came back, I got the key, and I left. That's all that happened."

"Do you know the mileage from your parents' house in Houston to their house at Lake Conroe?"

"Mileage?" Cody hesitated. "It's around forty-five miles, maybe forty-eight. It takes anywhere from an hour and twenty minutes to two hours to drive it, depending on traffic."

"How long did it take you last night?" Dad asked.

Cody sighed. "I'm not sure. I guess I was about forty minutes out when I remembered the key. Something like that."

"Accordin' to the way I figure," Bill Carlin drawled, "that means about forty goin' out plus forty comin' back. You left home at seven-thirty, so it looks like you got back here around eight-forty. Does that sound right to you?"

"I guess," Cody said. "But I wasn't home long. I picked up the house key and left right away."

"According to what you told me earlier, you decided not to stay at your lake house."

"That's right. I didn't. The air-conditioning wasn't working, so I took a sleeping bag outside on the deck."

"The police tried to contact you. They checked your lake house and couldn't find you."

"I—I left probably just before they got there. I

couldn't sleep. I had a lot on my mind. So I drove around the lake and parked in a quiet spot in the woods. I dozed off. When I woke up this morning, it was around five o'clock, so I drove back toward Houston."

"Did you stop anywhere?"

"Stop?"

"Did you buy gas, get something to eat? Is there anyone who might remember you being there?"

"I didn't need gas, but I did stop for doughnuts and coffee."

"Can you tell me where?"

"Somewhere . . . I don't know . . . I don't remember. There are lots of those little places off the highway." Cody's voice trembled as he added, "I know what you're thinking, but you've got to believe me! I didn't murder my parents!"

Chapter Four

Bill Carlin opened the gate. Cody followed him with Dad right behind. Dad saw me standing there, but he chose to ignore me.

"Cody," Bill drawled, "you got any relatives around here you can call on? A grandma, or an aunt and uncle? Any near kin?"

Cody's eyes were still wide and fearful, but Bill's question seemed to steady him, and a little color came back into his face. "My dad has . . . had no living relatives, but my mom's brother lives in Memorial, near Dairy Ashford."

"Name?"

"Oh. . . . Uncle . . . Frank . . . uh . . . Frank Baker."

"Well, you give me his phone number, and we'll get ahold of him and ask him to come on downtown to headquarters and meet us there."

"You're taking Cody to headquarters? You can't

arrest Cody!" I shouted. "It's not fair! I—you have to be fair!"

Bill shook his head slowly as he said to Dad, "Jake, you sure got a jumpy kid there." Then he turned to me and said, "Holly, nobody's talkin' about arrestin' anybody. There are a lot of questions to ask and answer. Cody wants us to catch whoever did this, and he's going to help us out."

As Bill went back into the house to make the call, Dad shot Cody the kind of look that used to make me cringe with guilt when I'd sneaked a cookie before dinner or forgotten a homework assignment. "Cody will help if he'll carefully think over exactly what happened and tell us the entire story—not just the parts that seem convenient."

Cody stared down at his feet. "I'm sorry. I was scared. It all sounded . . ." He took a deep breath and looked up, right at me. "I'll tell you the truth. I promise. Just please believe me."

"*I* believe you," I said.

Dad turned his gaze on me, and I thought I saw a glimmer of sympathy in his eyes. I certainly hoped so. "Just for the record, Holly," he said, "you're not going with us."

"Cody needs me."

"Cody has his uncle."

Cody's uncle. I'd never met him, but recently, while I was at Cody's for dinner, I had overheard his mom talking to his father.

"Frank called again today," she'd said with a voice that sounded somewhat disgusted, and Mr. Garnett muttered something I couldn't hear.

"I know, I know," she had said. "I told him you didn't want to hear about it, but you know Frank."

Cody had mentioned that his mom and Uncle Frank got along fine most of the time, but lately Frank was a topic that really bugged her.

"Frank looks down his nose at some of my dad's business deals," Cody'd said, "and Mom thinks he ought to mind his own business. But then Dad gets mad at Mom for telling Frank anything about them in the first place."

"What kind of deals is your father involved in?" I'd asked, realizing too late I shouldn't be so nosy.

Instead of telling me to mind my own business, as he had every right to do, Cody'd shrugged. "Dad invests in a lot of things. I don't really know many details." Cody had held out his hands and glanced around their elegant living room. "You can see that he does pretty well. I think it bugs Uncle Frank that Dad ignores his advice but keeps raking it in. Uncle Frank doesn't have as much as we do. At least it doesn't seem that he does."

Now I was worried. "Will your uncle come? Will he help you?" I asked Cody.

"I think so," Cody said. "He's my uncle, and he's always been friendly to me."

I glanced toward the street at the TV crews, who were shifting in Cody's direction, the neighborhood sightseers, and the yards of yellow police tape that ringed the Garnetts' property, and shivered. "Cody has to have a place to stay. He can't come back here, Dad," I said.

Dad clamped a reassuring hand on my shoulder. "We'll take care of Cody," he told me.

"I'm sure I can stay with my uncle," Cody said. "Don't worry, Holly. I didn't do anything wrong, so I'll be okay."

"Call me," I told him. "You said you needed a friend. I'm your friend. I'm here."

Cody shot a quick, almost fearful glance at Dad before he answered, "Thanks, Holly."

A plainclothes detective I didn't know came through the gate from the backyard. He held out a plastic bag to Dad. Inside the bag lay a black-and-white bone-handled knife that was smeared with dirt. "The top inch of the handle was protruding from the dirt under an oleander bush near the back fence," the detective said.

He didn't need to say what they were obviously thinking—that they'd found the murder weapon.

"That's one of our kitchen knives," Cody said. He stared at it as though he were hypnotized.

Bill returned, glanced at the knife, and nodded with satisfaction. "Almost too easy," he said to Dad, but he turned to Cody and his voice softened. "Your uncle's gonna meet us downtown," he said. "He was badly shook up, but he insists you're a good kid, Cody, and you couldn't have done it."

Cody looked as though he'd start crying again, so Dad hustled him off to his police car, and I didn't even get a chance to say goodbye.

I wandered to Mom's car, but just stood there as though I didn't know what to do next. I kept trying to think, but my thoughts were jumbled.

Cody didn't kill his parents. I knew he didn't. But I didn't know anything about investigating a crime, so how was I going to prove Cody's innocence?

"Ah. You're wearing amber."

Startled, I quickly looked around and saw a slightly built, dark-haired woman with skin the shade of Mom's real pearls. Her eyes were even darker than her hair, and they gave me the strange feeling that they were as deep as bottomless lakes. Her lips turned up in a smile.

"Amber?" I repeated. I had no idea what she was talking about.

"In your hair. Your barrette. It's real amber."

"Uh . . . yes," I said. As though I had to make sure, I reached up and touched the amber barrette with my fingertips. To my surprise, the stone pulsed with heat. Quickly I pulled my hand away and stared at my fingers.

"The barrette was a gift. My last birthday. From my mother," I babbled.

The woman gazed at me steadily for a moment. "You don't need to be afraid. I saw that you could feel the powers."

"Afraid?" I held my hands tightly together as all of what she had said began to register. "What . . . what powers?" I asked.

"Do you know about or understand the magical properties of amber?"

I took a step away. This woman made me nervous. "No—" I said, as she interrupted.

"Amber," she said calmly, "is a form of tree resin that was buried within the earth millions of years ago. It has absorbed the earth's energies and holds the earth's secrets. Those who wear amber have not chosen it; the amber has chosen them."

Even though what she was saying made me feel creepy, I couldn't resist asking, "Why?"

"Amber has mystical properties, and it calls to those who are sensitive enough to see and understand things in a dimension closed to most humans."

Slivers of ice prickled my backbone. I didn't need to hear this weird stuff. Not then. Not ever.

"I—I've got to go," I stammered. I pulled open the car door and jumped inside, slamming it with one hand as I turned on the ignition with the other. Cautiously I reached up to touch the amber stone in my barrette. It was smooth and barely warm. "I was standing in the sun," I told myself, and sighed with relief. "It was only the heat of the sun."

"If you need me—" the woman called, but I took off in a hurry and didn't hear the rest.

Why would I need her? For what? "She must be the neighborhood nut," I said aloud and tried to laugh, but the laugh didn't come. Instead, I kept remembering her dark eyes, and for just an instant I wished I had stayed to hear what she had tried to tell me.

S*aturday. 9:30* A.M. When I arrived home, I found Mom at the kitchen table, dressed in what she calls her "Saturday sloppies"—loose sweat pants, a baggy T-shirt, and sandals—but her strawberry blond hair was neatly brushed, and her skin glowed under a light cover of makeup. The Saturday morning editions of both the *Post* and *The Chronicle* were scattered over the table, along with toast crumbs, a dab of peach jam, and a pot of coffee.

The moment I came into the kitchen, Mom jumped to her feet, nearly upsetting her chair, and wrapped her arms around me.

"I'm sorry I took your car without asking," I said. "I had to be there when Cody came home."

"He's safe? He's all right?"

"Yes, and he needs me, Mom."

Mom murmured against my right ear, "It's okay, Holly. I understand. I'm not surprised that you insisted on being there when a friend needed you. I can't imagine you doing anything less."

I wasn't going to discuss the long-ago story of Paula. I just hugged Mom.

Mom moved back, holding me at arm's length as she studied my face. "Is Cody handling this all right? I know he's an only child, but are there any other relatives? Is there someone who can help him?"

I nodded. "He told me once that his father's parents died before he was born, and his mother's parents died when he was young, but he has an uncle who lives in Houston."

"Thank goodness."

Mom took a seat at the kitchen table and motioned toward the chair across from her. I could see the relief on her face dissolve and shift into a kind of watchful worry. "Holly," she said, "I need to know something about Cody."

Immediately I grew defensive. "Mom! Don't you believe him either?"

"You got the red-headed temperament from me." Her mouth twisted into a wry smile before she said, "Take it easy. I'm not accusing Cody of anything. In fact, because it means so much to you, I want to believe him. But I must know more about him. I know you've been friends for the last few years, and I've met his parents, but I don't really know much about what he's like, or what kind of a young man he's grown into, now that he's in high school."

I forced myself to calm down. Mom was right. I suppose I'd feel the same way in her place. "Cody gets good grades, and he's got a terrific sense of humor, and we like a lot of the same things."

"How about his friends? What do you think of them?"

"There are three guys he hangs out with, and they're okay, but I don't know any of them very well. They weren't in my classes when we were younger."

I realized, as soon as the words were out, that wasn't a very smart thing to say, but Mom didn't pick up on it. She thought a moment, then asked, "Exactly how much do you like Cody?"

My face grew hot. "Mom," I complained, "talking about how much you like a guy is girl talk. It's not the kind of thing you discuss with your mother."

"Then why don't you pretend I'm Sara?"

I took a good, long look at Mom and said, "I can't."

Mom got up, poured herself a cup of coffee, and sat down again. She took a careful sip of the coffee and asked, "Is it puppy love, Holly?"

I scowled. "See? That's what I mean. There's no such thing as 'puppy love.' Teenagers have feelings too. If you care about a guy, it's real. Sometimes it's great, and sometimes it hurts. The feelings are there, and it's not something for grown-ups to put down. Don't you remember when you were a teenager? Wasn't there some guy you liked? Can't you remember how it felt?"

Mom thought a moment, and when she spoke, her voice was sad. "That was a long, long time ago."

"There's 'in love' and there's 'in like,' " I said. "I like Cody a lot, Mom. I have ever since we were kids. It's not love yet. It's still 'in like,' but I care a lot about him. Someday . . . well, who knows? Someday I may fall in love with him. Right now . . . right now he needs me."

"Thank you. You gave me an honest answer," Mom said. "Now I have something else to ask you." Her eyes never left my face. Even when she took a sip of coffee, she peered at me over the rim of the cup.

Finally she put down the cup and asked, "You heard what your father had to say about the crime, and you've talked to Cody. Do you honestly, truthfully, one hundred percent believe that he had nothing to do with the murders of his parents?"

I hesitated, then instantly regretted it. I hadn't immediately defended Paula when I'd had the chance, but of course then I'd been a witness and only needed a second to reply. "Yes," I answered firmly, my voice so loud that it filled the kitchen. "Cody had nothing to do with the murders."

"Then I'll go along with your decision," Mom said. "All I ask is that you use good judgment in what you do."

"Thanks, Mom," I said.

She sighed. "I don't know what's happened to our world. Over and over, in the newspapers and on television news we read and hear about robberies that turn to murder—but we don't believe it could happen to anyone we know."

"Robbery?" I asked. "Dad didn't say anything about this being a robbery too."

Mom went to the table and flipped through the newspaper until she found the local-news section of the *Post* and handed it to me. "It's in the newspapers. Mr. Garnett's wallet is missing, and Mrs. Garnett's purse and some of her jewelry."

A robbery! That proved it couldn't have been Cody! Dad would have figured that out right away. That meant Cody really *was* being questioned only to help the police find the murderer, just as Bill had said. I dropped into the nearest chair, suddenly hungry and so relieved that I wanted to shout.

Mom scrambled an egg for me and made some

toast, and I downed a huge glass of orange juice, while I read what both newspapers had printed about the murder.

Besides telling about the robbery, the articles had a brief mention of a neighbor discovering the bodies. *Poor Mr. Arlington,* I thought. He had been so afraid.

I winced as I read that Mr. and Mrs. Garnett had died from multiple stab wounds. "It's usually great anger or drugs behind this type of killing," the crime scene investigator was quoted as saying.

I knew the Homicide Division investigator, Luis Martinez, and, because of what Dad had explained to Mom and me, I knew how the system worked.

The first officer to arrive on a murder scene secures the scene and calls in the report. Luis is then sent to the scene. He talks with the first officer, taking note of all the facts and the officer's own opinions. Then, after Luis conducts a careful preliminary examination of the scene, he alerts the medical examiner's office and calls the lieutenant in Homicide to tell him what he's found. At that point at least one team of homicide detectives is dispatched to the scene. Sometimes more, depending on what they call "media elevation," which means how big a story it's going to be in the newspapers and on TV. In this case the primary homicide detectives were Dad and Bill Carlin.

While Dad and Bill carry on their investigation, tracking down every lead and talking to witnesses, Luis takes measurements, draws sketches, gets fingerprints or even footprints, and collects fibers, hair, and any other items, no matter how tiny, that might have a significance. Luis told me once that sometimes he works for hours on his hands and knees, covering every square inch of a room. One tiny fleck of blue yarn, for instance, can match the sweater of a suspect and show that he was at the scene of the crime, no matter what he insists.

I shivered as it dawned on me that Cody's fingerprints, hair, and threads from his clothing would be all over the house because he lived there. What if the crime lab couldn't find traces the murderer had unknowingly left behind in the Garnetts' house?

Stop thinking like that! I told myself. *They have to!*

Chapter Five

I finished reading the newspaper reports and pushed back my chair just as the back door opened and Dad came in. The circles under his eyes were deeper, and his entire body sagged like a leaking balloon.

As he pulled out a chair, Mom asked, "Jake, you must be hungry. Would you like eggs and toast?" She glanced at the clock. "Or lunch. How about a sandwich?"

Dad shook his head. "No thanks, Lynn. I had some coffee and doughnuts."

"Caffeine and sugar," Mom said, the corners of her mouth turned down in disgust. "Let me make you something substantial."

"I said I don't want anything!" He caught the sharpness in his own voice and mumbled, "Sorry. I guess what I need most is a bath and some sleep."

"Let's hope they improve your disposition."

Mom's lips became a thin line, drawn with a pencil, but before Dad could react, I quickly said, "I read about the robbery. You didn't tell me that the Garnetts were robbed. The robbery is why they were murdered. Right?"

Dad shook his head. "Money, credit cards, some jewelry? It wasn't enough."

"What does that mean?"

"Among other things there were sterling silver candlesticks and a tea set on the sideboard, a framed coin collection that's got to be valuable, and a computer and printer in Garnett's office. Someone who'd kill in order to steal what he wanted would have gone after the big pieces."

Bewildered, I said, "I still don't understand."

"I'm saying, Holly, that the so-called robbery could have been staged to make us think that a stranger had come into the house and committed the murder."

"You don't think so."

"No, I don't. There'd be no reason for a stranger to exhibit the anger that was shown in the multiple stabbings."

"You have the murder weapon. Don't the prints tell you anything?"

"Funny thing about that knife," Dad said. "It's from an expensive knife set, so I can't imagine what it was doing buried in the backyard."

"Because it's the murder weapon."

"No it isn't," Dad said.

"It has to be. Just because the murderer wiped off the prints—"

"Holly," Dad interrupted, "the knife was wiped

clean of prints, that's true. But there was no blood on it."

"He would have wiped the blood off too."

"There's no way he would have succeeded. The crime lab has chemicals now that can find the tiniest trace of blood caught in a crevice and even show where blood has once been. We're looking for the real weapon right now in Dumpsters, ditches, alleys—anywhere from here to Lake Conroe, where the weapon might have been tossed."

"Dad!" I wailed, horrified at what he was say-ing. "You still think Cody had something to do with the murder! How could you?"

"Because it fits the pattern we find in most cases like this," he said.

"This isn't most cases!" Desperately I said, "And Cody isn't the only surviving relative. What about his uncle, Frank?"

"You're reaching," Dad said.

"But it's possible," I insisted. "Cody told me that his uncle criticized his dad's business invest-ments."

Dad raised one eyebrow. "That's a motive for murder?"

"Okay," I said. "I'm just trying to look at every possibility. You've told us more than once that a good investigator has to keep an open mind."

"That's right, and I am keeping an open mind."

"No you're not! You keep talking about usual cases. This isn't a usual case. This is different."

Dad sighed and slid down in his chair, stretching out his legs and nudging off his shoes. "Right now I don't want to talk about it," he told me.

"But I do!"

"Holly . . . ," Mom said. "It's obvious that your father's in no mood to discuss this right now, and you didn't get much sleep last night. Go upstairs to bed, turn off the phone in your room, and try to catch up."

I pushed back my chair and carried my dirty dishes to the sink. "You're wrong about Cody, and I'm going to prove it, Dad," I said before I left the kitchen.

"Holly," Dad said, "you don't know what you're talking about. You don't know the facts."

"I know that Cody is innocent, so I'm going to do what you should be doing—trying to prove it."

"That's not my job," Dad said. "My job is to investigate everyone and everything until I uncover the truth."

He put both hands over his face, his fingertips rubbing at his forehead as if it hurt and he could rub the pain away. Mom was right. There was no use trying to talk to Dad now.

But as soon as I left the room, I heard Mom's voice tighten. "Cody is Holly's friend, Jake," she said. "Naturally she's frightened about what has happened, and she's terribly worried about Cody. You could have given her some encouragement. She's your daughter and needs your help. Or are you going to tell me that's not your job either?"

"Lynn, after all these years I'd expect you to understand something about the work I do and how I have to do it."

59

"Oh, I understand, all right. I understand that your job comes first and your wife and daughter are either a far second or don't make the list at all."

I didn't hear what Dad said next. I ran up the stairs to my room, wishing with all my heart that things could be different, that all the happy years I knew when I was little could be stretched out to last forever.

Instead, with their constant, painful jabs at each other, Mom and Dad were stabbing their marriage to death.

S*aturday. 2:15 P.M.* I woke up from a heavy sleep, surprised that I'd been able to nap. I took a shower, dressed in blue shorts with a matching striped top, and came downstairs. I sat in a broad patch of late afternoon sunlight that poured through the west window of the den and brushed my hair dry in its warmth.

Mom came into the room, stopped for just a moment, then smiled. "With the sun highlighting your hair, you look as though you're wearing a halo of fire."

I put down my hairbrush, tucked my hair into my amber barrette, and looked up. "I'm sorry I caused so much trouble, Mom. I didn't mean to create problems between you and Dad."

"It's not your fault." She turned away to stare out the window.

Before I'd fallen asleep, I'd thought of so many things I could say to my parents to convince Dad he should pay more attention to Mom and to show Mom how she could be more patient with Dad. But now my mind was as empty as a cereal bowl with only little crumbles of thoughts swimming around in the bottom. "Listen to me, Mom—" I began, hoping that if I just started talking, I'd remember what I'd planned to say.

Mom interrupted. She spoke slowly, as though the words had a bad taste. "Before I forget, Cody telephoned, but you were in the shower. I talked to him, and I spoke with his uncle. I told Cody you'd call back."

"Oh!"

She frowned and added, "He gave me his uncle's telephone number and address. It's written on the pad next to the kitchen phone. He asked if you'd call Cody as soon as possible, but I'm not sure it's a good idea."

"Mom, you're as bad as Dad, taking it for granted Cody's guilty," I cried. "I can talk to him, can't I? Can't I, please?"

I waited agonies of time until Mom finally nodded agreement. I ran to the kitchen. My fingers trembled as I dialed the number.

Cody's uncle answered the phone, and we made polite remarks to each other before he called Cody to the phone.

Cody's voice was strained and shaky. "You said you'd come over," he blurted out. "Did you mean it?"

"I meant it."

"I can't come to you. The police impounded my car so they can check it out."

61

I should have expected that. They'd look for the murder weapon, for traces of blood. . . . I shuddered. "Do you want me to come now?" I asked.

"Yes."

I thought about Mom's attitude. Would she let me visit Cody? I seriously doubted it, but I was determined to give it my best try. "I'll check with Mom," I told Cody. If she gives her okay, I'll be at your uncle's house within twenty minutes."

As I walked into the den, the phone rang again. Mom reached for it and said, "Hi, Sara. Yes, she's right here," and handed the receiver to me.

Just the sound of Sara's name brought the comfort I remembered from snuggling my old teddy bear. Sara Madison, my best friend, who's two inches shorter than I am, at five feet four, and roundly plump in both the right and wrong places, wouldn't like being compared to a teddy bear.

Sara is one of four kids in a very busy, very noisy family. A lot of that noise comes from laughter. Sometimes, when I'm at the Madisons' house for dinner, wrapped inside a tornado of teasing and joking, and shouts of "Hey, listen to me!" competing with the baby's happy yells as she bangs on the high-chair tray, I get a little jealous. I'm not proud of being jealous of my best friend. Sometimes I hate myself for it. But even when one of the kids is getting scolded, there's so much love in that house I can feel it, and I want that same kind of love to come back to *my* house again.

As soon as I said hello, Sara cried out, "Holly. I

read about it, and I'm so sorry! What can I do to help?"

"I knew you'd say that," I told her, so grateful that tears came to my eyes.

"That's what friends are for."

"Cody isn't the murderer," I said.

Sara didn't ask a lot of questions, and she didn't argue with me. She just said, "Okay, so tell me. What can I do to help you?"

"I need to talk," I said. Mom was watching, and it made me uncomfortable, so I turned my back. "Later," I told her. "Okay?"

"Sure," Sara said. "Just give me a call."

I hung up and turned to Mom. "May I use your car—just for a little while?"

"Of course," Mom said.

She didn't ask where I was going. I realized that she took it for granted I wanted to see Sara. If I told her I was going to Cody . . . ? No. I couldn't take the chance. I fought back a pang of guilt, snatched up Mom's extra car keys, and dashed out the door.

*F*rank Baker's house wasn't hard to find. It was in a quiet subdivision, which was bracketed by two sets of large, busy shopping centers. Light brick, with a beige-painted trim, the house blended in with its neighbors, probably all built at the same time with nearly identical floor plans. Same trees in front, same flower beds, same thick carpets of St. Augustine grass—each arranged just differently enough to stamp a slight individual touch.

I was startled when Mr. Baker answered the door. I expected to see an older man, maybe dark haired, maybe balding; but Frank Baker looked as though he was in his mid-thirties. His blond hair had been bleached by the sun, and his tan was dusted with a light burn that gave it a reddish glow. Tall and good-looking, he wore a T-shirt and shorts, and was barefoot.

"So you're Holly," he said and smiled warmly. "Cody has good taste."

Embarrassed, and puzzled because I expected soft words and an expression of mourning, I stammered, "I—I'm t-terribly sorry about your sister and . . . and . . ."

My face must have mirrored my thoughts. My voice trailed away like a worn-out tape, but Mr. Baker nodded as though I'd said exactly the right thing and took my arm.

"Nelda's and Sam's deaths are a terrible tragedy. An unbelievable tragedy," he said. "But life has to go on. It's Cody's life that's important now, and it wouldn't help him a bit if I let go with all my own hurt and anger. Cody's my nephew. I love him, and I've got to stay strong for him."

Mr. Baker led me into the house as he added, "Cody's waiting for you in the den. I'm glad you could come. You can imagine how he's feeling."

The wood-paneled den was dimly lit, its drapes across the sliding glass doors closed to keep out the hot sunlight. Cody, who was seated on a low sofa, raised his head from his hands. "Holly," he said. "You came."

He unfolded himself from the sofa like an arthritic old man, and, as he walked toward me, I cringed at the pain in his eyes.

"I told you I'd come." Impulsively I stepped forward and hugged him, heedless of Mr. Baker, who dropped into a nearby easy chair.

"How about a soft drink, Holly? Or orange juice? I've got a box of assorted English cookies, if you'd like."

"No thank you, Mr. Baker," I said, wishing he would go away.

"Call me Frank," he told me and flashed his brilliant smile again.

"I'd like some orange juice," Cody said.

"And something to eat, I hope," Frank said.

"No. I'm not hungry. I'm thirsty. I keep getting so thirsty."

I followed Cody to the kitchen, which was deadly dull in beige tile, beige counters, beige-painted cabinets—even beige curtains at the window. The only relief to this sea of blandness was a cluttered array of cooking tools hanging on the wall every which way, from ladles, spoons, a knife set, and sieves, to those copper-bottom pans that have to be polished. It looked as though Frank liked to cook, but his taste in decorating would give anyone a headache.

I didn't like being in this room. Something about it—maybe all that disordered mess on the walls—made me uncomfortable, so I was glad when Cody finished pouring his glass of orange juice, then led me back to the den and to the sofa.

He clutched my hand so tightly I felt nervous tremors tingle from his body into mine. "The police think I did it." Cody's voice was low.

"No they don't," I lied. "Detectives keep their minds open to all possibilities. They look for the truth."

Cody didn't answer, and Frank raised one eyebrow.

"Okay," I said. "I know it sounds nerdy, but that's what my dad's told me over and over. That's what he does."

"In any case," Frank said, "the three of us know that Cody didn't commit the murders, so even though the circumstantial evidence looks bad, we'll beat it."

"There's not that much evidence against Cody, is there?" I could hear the hope in my voice. "Just because he came back to the house . . . well, he had a good reason. He'd forgotten the key to the lake house."

"I wish I'd told them about it in the first place," Cody mumbled. "That and the argument." His eyes scrunched up in torment. "I wish I'd had enough sense to have told them, myself, about the argument."

Chapter Six

I twisted to face Cody. "What argument?"

Frank leaned forward, resting his forearms on his knees. He winced as he said, "Look, Cody, before we were interrogated, we'd said to each other, 'Tell the truth, and we'll have nothing to worry about.' Right? So how'd I know that you hadn't told the detectives about the argument with your parents? When they asked me what I knew about your relationship, I told them what Sam and Nelda told me."

I grew so cold and so scared it was hard to speak. "Tell me about the argument," I said to Cody.

Cody's shoulders hunched around his ears as though he could hide inside them, like a turtle in his shell. When he didn't answer immediately, Frank said, "It wasn't anything special. It was the kind of argument about money kids often have with their parents."

"Money?" I asked. Cody's parents seemed to have plenty of money. I'd thought Cody had everything he needed or wanted.

When Cody didn't say anything, Frank filled me in. "Cody wanted money for a new car."

Cody suddenly lifted his head. "Every cent I get goes into repairs on the Thunderbird. It has over one hundred thousand miles on it, and it's going to need major work. I talked to Mom and Dad about it a dozen times, but I couldn't get through to them."

"That doesn't sound like an argument to me," I said. "It sounds like nothing more than a discussion."

"It was . . . sort of," Cody said, "until Friday night. I got kind of upset. Kind of . . . well, mad that they wouldn't listen. I told them I'd work. I'd pay them back."

Frank sighed. "I wish that was all you told them. I wish you hadn't come back and yelled at them that you'd show them, that you'd get the money somewhere, somehow."

"I didn't mean it the way it sounds. I was angry. I just said things without thinking. Dad wouldn't let go. He wouldn't end the argument."

"Did you witness the argument?" I asked Frank. I sounded so much like an investigator that I blushed. Well, maybe I had the right to be an investigator. I'd told Dad I'd prove that Cody was innocent, and I had to start somewhere.

"No," he said. "I dropped by for a few minutes

after Cody had just left, a few minutes after seven-thirty. Both Sam and Nelda were so steamed by the argument with Cody that they sounded off and told me all about it. They lived well, but that was mostly because of Nelda's half of the inheritance after our mother died. Sam is . . . was always pretty tight with a dollar and wasn't about to shell out for a new car for Cody when he thought the old car had a couple of good years left in it."

Tears rolled down Cody's cheeks, and his shoulders heaved as he gave a deep, shuddering sob. "I wish I'd never said anything about a car!" he cried and beat a fist against the arm of the sofa. "It's all so stupid!"

"That's why you were upset and couldn't sleep?" I asked.

"What are we talking about here?" Frank asked.

"Why the police couldn't find Cody at the lake house. Cody said he took a sleeping bag out on the deck to sleep, but he had a lot on his mind and couldn't sleep, so he drove around the lake and finally went to sleep in his car in the woods."

Frank looked kind of sick. "Oh, Cody, Cody," he said and slowly shook his head.

"I didn't know there'd be any problem with what I was doing," Cody mumbled. "I was upset, and I was angry. I just didn't know."

I moved to put my arms around Cody, but Frank got to his feet and said, "Holly, I think what Cody needs most right now is some food and some rest."

69

Cody didn't answer, so I stood up too. "And a lawyer," I said. "Did you get him a lawyer?"

A smile briefly touched Frank's lips. "You sound like your father. That's just what he asked. And the answer is, yes. Before Cody was questioned, I hired a criminal defense attorney who sat in on the session. Paul Ormond and I work out together. He handles lots of defense cases, and he's got a good reputation. Okay?"

I nodded and tried to smile in return. "Now if the police can just find the man who Mr. Arlington saw jumping the back fences . . ."

"What man? Who did Mr. Arlington see?" Cody slowly got to his feet, staring at me intently.

"Oh," I said. "You don't remember that I told you. You were still pretty much out of it."

"Tell me again, Holly," Cody said.

"Sure." I took a long breath, speaking quickly. "Mr. Arlington told Dad and the reporters that he saw a tall, muscular guy jump the back fences. He apparently came from the Garnetts' yard into his, then climbed over the back fence into the yard of the people who live behind Mr. Arlington. He was probably headed for a car parked on the next street. The women who live in the house behind Mr. Arlington's said their dog barked at him."

Frank looked as surprised as Cody. "The police didn't tell us that."

"They probably wouldn't," I said. "They wouldn't have any reason to."

"It would have made us feel a lot better," Cody said. He stood a little taller. "Could Mr. Arlington identify the man he saw?"

"No. He said it was too dark to make out clothing or features."

They both looked so disappointed I quickly added, "Dad said they were checking it out. They'll hunt for fingerprints or threads that might have caught on the boards, or footprints in the area—there's a lot of evidence that most people wouldn't even think about that detectives look for. And they'll talk to people on that street to see if anyone saw the guy."

Frank clapped Cody on the shoulder. "There you go," he said. "We've got things working for us that we didn't even know about. Things are looking up, Cody."

"Yeah," Cody said and, for the first time, seemed more like the strong, confident Cody I knew. "Come on, Holly. I'll walk you to your car."

"Come back soon, Holly," Frank said, "and keep us posted about what's going on. Okay?"

"I will," I said, but I waited until Cody and I were out of Frank's hearing before I said, "I'm going to prove that you're innocent."

Cody looked down and smiled at me teasingly. "You? All by yourself?"

"No. You're going to help me."

Cody gave me a quick hug. "You don't know what a relief it is to find out that Mr. Arlington saw the murderer. I hope that it doesn't take the police very long to find out who he is and catch him."

"They don't have much to go on, so we may have to help."

"How?"

"I wish I knew," I said. "But don't worry. We'll do it."

His smile vanished as he said, "I feel awful about that argument with my parents. And I'm sorry you had to know about it. Sometimes it was hard to talk with my parents. Sometimes I blew it. Dad had a temper. I do too. You probably don't understand what that's like—"

"Sometimes I yell too," I interrupted. "I don't like it when I do, but Dad can make me so mad . . . " I broke off and shrugged. "Hey, everybody sounds off once in a while."

Cody didn't answer, so I said, "Why don't you do what your uncle told you to do—eat something and get some sleep? We'll get past all this. I promise."

"I'll never get over it, Holly," Cody said. "Not ever."

I live in Bellaire, a nice community surrounded by the city of Houston. And it's got a good high school—Bellaire High—which is where Cody and I met. The easiest way for me to get from Frank Baker's suburb, in what's called the Memorial area, was to take I-10 to the 610 loop, but I surprised myself by heading off the loop just past the Galleria area onto the Southwest Freeway, heading north, instead of following the loop into Bellaire. I knew I should go home and return Sara's call but, instead, I swung off the freeway at the Kirby exit and drove down to the street on which the Garnetts lived.

The street was shaded with large, overhanging trees, and carefully designed and tended front gardens splashed the edges of the thick lawns with wild late summer color. At this—the warmest part of the day—everyone was indoors. I pulled up in front of the Garnetts' house and parked.

The yellow crime tape had been removed, and the house faced its neighbors with a gracious and elegant neatness, so carefully guarding its secrets that no one could guess at the horror that had taken place inside.

But someone who lived on the block might not be so secretive. Someone might have seen the man Mr. Arlington had seen. Someone might know someone who could help Cody. I knew that Dad and Bill would contact all the neighbors, if they hadn't already; but still there might be something one of the neighbors would think of later. It wouldn't hurt to ask.

There was no point in talking to Mr. Arlington, so I began with the large house on the other side of the Garnetts'. A well-dressed, middle-aged man opened the door.

"Hi," I said. "I'm Holly Campbell."

"Sorry, Holly," he said as he fished out his wallet, removed a dollar, and thrust it at me. "I haven't got time for a raffle-ticket spiel. Put this toward your school fund or whatever you're collecting for."

"I'm not collecting money for anything," I said and waved the dollar away. "I'm investigating a murder."

For an instant his mouth fell open. Then he

started to chuckle. "Houston's youngest under-cover cop?"

"I'm Cody Garnett's friend," I said. "Cody and I are trying to find out who killed his parents."

He raised an eyebrow. "From what I read in the newspaper, Cody could use an attorney more than an investigator. I assume he has one?"

My face burned. "Cody's innocent. I'm trying to prove it. And he does have an attorney."

"May I ask who is representing Cody?"

"Paul Ormond. He's a friend of Cody's uncle."

One eyebrow rose again. "I know Mr. Or-mond," the man said. "In this case I suppose he'll do."

"Are you an attorney too?"

"Civil cases only, not criminal." He began to shut the door, but I fought back my anger and begged, "Please, just answer two questions for me? Were you home last night between eight and ten?"

"The estimated time of the murder? Yes. My wife and I were at home."

"Did you hear anything at the Garnetts' house? Like loud music?"

"We didn't hear a thing. The air-conditioning units serve to insulate us from most outside noises."

"Did you see anyone come to the Garnetts' house during that time?"

"You said *two* questions. I answered them." The man shut the door quietly but firmly.

I turned and walked to the sidewalk, discour-agement settling like a hard lump in my stomach. I stopped long enough to take a deep breath and stand up a little straighter before I approached the next house. So the first person I'd met was rude. So what? Maybe the people in this house would want to help.

But a woman dressed in a white uniform peered at me through the lead-glass pane, then opened the huge front door. The marble-tiled entry hall smelled of stale flowers and antiseptic soap.

"I'm sorry," the woman said when I told her what I wanted. "There's only Mr. Plotz here. He's not only bedridden; he's practically stone-deaf."

"Were you here? Did you see anyone come to the Garnetts' house? Did you hear anything?"

"No. I was watching the TV in Mr. Plotz's room until close to midnight. I'm sorry, but I can't help you."

"Thanks," I said and walked back to the sidewalk, trying to think. The rest of the block on this side of the street consisted of three more of the elegant houses, which sat smugly in a row as though knowing they were special. The people who lived in them weren't likely to have seen or heard anything. The people who lived across the street, who could see the Garnetts' house from their front windows—they would be the ones to ask. Mrs. Marsh lived directly across from the Garnetts, but I'd already heard what she had to say about seeing Cody leave the house twice. I didn't want to hear it again.

Next to Mrs. Marsh's house was a lot shaded by at least a dozen pines and oaks, and tucked into this well of coolness was a neat little yellow brick house. With its blue front door and scrolled trim bordering the windows, it could have passed for the witch's house in "Hansel and Gretel." All it needed was a row of candy canes marching up to the doorway.

But how much could the people who lived there see from behind all those trees? I'd probably do better trying the house on the other side of the Marsh home—one of the "large lovelies," as I was beginning to think of them. My mind made up, I took a few steps, then stopped, my gaze pulled again to the "Hansel and Gretel" house.

No, I thought, and started down the block, but stopped again, drawn toward the little house under the trees. Okay. I was here, so I'd try the little house first. Even if the occupants of the house hadn't seen or heard anything, it made sense not to leave them out.

The walk wasn't another straight line from sidewalk to front steps. It wound back and forth in curves as round as a garden snake's, carrying me into a silent, sheltered, green-spun world that was perfumed with a damp, earthy, mossy fragrance.

As I reached the front door, it opened, and the woman who stood there in the dusky light smiled. It wasn't a smile of welcome but a satisfied smile she had saved for herself.

"The girl with amber in her hair," she murmured. "I knew you would come."

Chapter Seven

Her hair was as jet black as I remembered it, her skin pearly, even in the greenish light. She was dressed in a plain white T-shirt and jeans, but around her neck, on a chain, hung an orb of amber, glimmering with golden lights.

As I stood there, gaping, the woman stepped aside and said, "Please come in."

"Oh . . . thanks, but I can't," I answered. "I just want . . ."

"You want to ask me some questions. Come in. I may be able to answer them for you."

She beckoned and, feeling as though I had no choice, I followed her into the living room. It was decorated in soft blues and greens, touched here and there with the subdued sunlight that filtered through the trees. As the door closed behind me, sealing off this underwaterlike aquarium, I settled into a chair. The rippling colors washed over and through me.

"My name is Glenda Jordan," the woman said as she sat on a hassock opposite me. "Please call me Glenda."

"I'm Holly Campbell."

"You sought me out, Holly, so that I—"

"Actually," I cut in, "I'm going to as many houses as I can on the street, trying to find someone who might have seen or heard something at the Garnetts' last night."

"You sought me out," she repeated.

There was no point in arguing, so I asked, "Did you see anyone besides Cody come or go from the Garnetts' house?"

"Physically," she said, "I did not see anyone."

I must have looked as bewildered as I felt, because Glenda leaned forward, stared into my eyes with those deep pools of black, and murmured, "Let me explain. I see what others may not see, Holly. I am a clairvoyant."

"What's a clairvoyant? Is it like a psychic?" I asked nervously. I wasn't too sure what a psychic was either.

Glenda gave a little shake of her head. "No, no." She picked up an egg-shaped polished stone that lay on her coffee table and held it out. "A psychic might take an object like this, something that belonged to an individual, and try to make mental contact with that person."

Suddenly remembering, I said, "I've read about that. A psychic in Dallas goes through this routine when she works with the police in finding missing bodies."

"I'm aware of her work."

"And some psychics claim to tell the future, don't they?"

Glenda frowned. "No matter what anyone claims, no one can foretell the future. It is not for us to know."

"You don't believe in horoscopes?"

"No. I do not."

Puzzled, I said, "You haven't told me yet what a clairvoyant is."

"A clairvoyant is someone who has the power to see objects, people, or actions removed from natural viewing."

"I don't understand."

"A clairvoyant deals directly with the spirits, through visions. A clairvoyant is a spirit seeker." When I didn't respond, she said, "At times I get a direct picture of an event taking place. It's like a motion picture in my mind. This is why we need to talk about the Garnetts' murder."

A shiver ran up my backbone. "What are you telling me? That you saw . . ." I gulped and started over, my voice quivering. "Are you saying that you *saw* the murder across the street in your mind?"

"Some of it," she said. "Only that which I was allowed to see."

I stood up, my knees so wobbly I could hardly stand. What was I doing in this house with this strange woman? "Uh . . . maybe you should tell the police," I said.

Glenda stood and put a hand on my arm. I wanted to run, but I couldn't leave. I couldn't even move. "As I told you, I saw only some of what took place in the house that night," she said. A look of horror shivered across her face, and I waited, unable to breathe, until she composed herself. "Unfortunately," she added, "I did not see the face of the murderer."

Frantically I pulled away and edged toward the front door. "Well, maybe," I suggested, wishing I were anyplace but there, "you should think some more about it and . . ."

"I have thought about it," she said. "I'm sorry I couldn't have captured the entire scene in my mind, even though it would be excruciatingly hard to bear. But there is another route to discovery. To succeed, I would need to visit the Garnetts' house."

I stumbled backward, toward the front door. "Uh . . . you'll have to talk to Cody or his uncle or maybe the police about that."

Her dark eyes drilled into mine as she said, "I would like to visit the house with *you*."

My elbow banged against the door, and I winced as I groped for the knob. "No. Not with me," I said.

"Yes," she insisted. "With you, because you are an amber person. Because you have the power and the gifts."

My fingers reached the knob, and I tugged, but it wouldn't open. Desperately I said, "I don't! Really, I don't!"

"Hush," Glenda said. "Listen. Relax. Just open

your mind and listen. I have something to tell you."

Maybe it was the depth of her dark eyes, maybe I was just so frightened I couldn't fight another minute, or maybe it was the musical softness of her voice. I leaned against the door, shut out the jumble of thoughts that had been jolting like electric sparks through my mind, and listened.

Don't be afraid of what you can do, Glenda said.

"I'm not afraid," I answered defensively.

"I didn't speak aloud," Glenda told me, and I realized with a shock that she was right. I'd been looking right at her, and her lips hadn't moved.

"I heard the words in my mind. How did that happen?"

"Telepathy," Glenda answered my question. "Amber girl, we were able to communicate through our minds."

"No!" Suddenly the world jerked back into focus. I turned my back on Glenda, flipped the dead bolt away from the door, and threw it open.

As I pulled off my amber barrette, my hair tumbled across my forehead. The barrette burned my fingers, and I wished I could throw it away, but I couldn't. It was my most valuable possession—a smooth, gleaming oval of amber set in a silver filigree frame—and I treasured it because Mom had given it to me.

"It doesn't matter if you wear the amber or not," Glenda said. "The amber has already recognized your power. As I told you, the stone is mystical and calls to those who can respond."

"Look . . . I didn't buy the barrette. My mom did."

"No matter how it came into your possession, it was meant to be yours," Glenda said. "Come back when you're ready, Holly. I'll be here waiting."

Gasping for breath, I ran as fast as I could down the twisting path and across the street. I jumped into Mom's car, turned on the ignition with fingers so shaky they could hardly hold on to the key, and drove away fast.

I drove straight home. Glenda Jordan scared me to death!

When I burst into the house, I found Mom in the den, correcting her fourth-graders' math papers. She looked up in surprise as I flopped into the nearest chair.

"Good heavens, Holly! What happened to your hair?"

"I took out my barrette."

"You didn't lose it, did you?"

In answer I held out the barrette so Mom could see it. The amber glowed with a warm, soft light, and the silver filigree glittered in the light from Mom's reading lamp.

"It's beautiful, isn't it?" Mom said and smiled.

"It's gorgeous." As I stared at it, I told myself, *It's nothing more than a barrette. What am I afraid of?* Calmly I pulled back the tangle of hair that was hanging in front of my eyes and tucked it firmly into the barrette. "How'd you happen to buy it, Mom?" I asked, trying to make my question sound casual.

"As a matter of fact," Mom said, "I had planned to buy you a beautiful gold-colored sweater that would have really set off your red hair. For some reason, while I was waiting my turn for a saleswoman, I spotted a display of jewelry on a nearby counter. I have no idea what made me walk across the aisle to look at the jewelry, but when I saw that barrette . . . well, it almost jumped into my hand. I knew it would be perfect for you."

"It called to you," I whispered, shaken again.

"Well, I suppose if you want to be whimsical, you could say that." She bent to her papers, then looked up again. "You do like the barrette, don't you, Holly?"

"I love it," I answered. So-called mystical powers or not, I really, truly did.

*T*en minutes after I telephoned, Sara came over. After we were squirreled away in my bedroom, I really let it all out.

Sara tried to comfort me. "In this country you're innocent until proven guilty. I told my dad the same thing. It's going to be okay, Holly."

"You're saying that your dad thinks Cody did it?"

"He's just going by what's on the TV news and in the papers."

"It's not fair!" I punched at the bed pillow I was holding on my lap. "Reporters are making everyone think the wrong thing."

"They're just giving the facts," Sara said calmly, "and face it, Holly, the facts don't look good. Cody left his house twice, the second time close to when the murder probably took place. He said he was going to stay at the lake house, but when the police looked for him there, they couldn't find him."

"Cody told them why. He gave them perfectly good reasons." I didn't tell Sara that Cody had changed his story, and I hadn't told her about his argument with his parents. I didn't want to add anything that would make her question Cody's innocence.

I hugged the pillow to my chest and rested my chin on the edge. "Dad said in most family murders where there's one member left alive, the police find that remaining member committed the murder. He's prejudiced against Cody, just because of some dumb statistics."

"Don't get mad at your dad. He's a good detective. He'll be fair."

I sighed. "Sara, I told Dad I was going to prove that Cody didn't do it. I talked to some neighbors, and that didn't help. Two of them said they didn't see or hear anything. The third—are you ready for this?—said she was clairvoyant and saw the murders take place in her mind. It was really weird." I shivered as I pictured Glenda's face. When I was at her house, she had picked up my thoughts. What if she were tuning in to them now? I felt myself blush.

Sara didn't notice. She frowned. "If she's a clairvoyant who really saw what happened, as she claims, she should be able to identify the murderer."

"She said she didn't see that part."

"Then you're right. She's weird and a fake and just wants people to think she's important. Or maybe she wants publicity."

I left it at that. The amber, and the strange things Glenda had said about its powers, seemed too bizarre to talk about with anyone, even Sara.

"Why don't you ask your dad to share his information with you?"

"You mean like the medical examiner's report and the crime lab report?"

She nodded.

I smiled and asked, "How do you know about all that stuff?"

"I watch detective shows on TV." Sara grinned.

"I wonder if Dad really would answer my questions," I mused.

"Try it," Sara answered. "It won't hurt to ask him."

S*aturday. 7:10 P.M.* Mom and I had dinner alone. Dad didn't show up until around eleven. I remember when Mom used to wait up for him. She'd make him something to eat and sit with him, sometimes just listening as he sounded off about the problems he was running into, letting him get some of the pressures of his job off his chest.

But lately Mom would trot upstairs to bed, pretending to sleep, by the time Dad got home.

This time she got up from her chair before the ten o'clock news began and gathered up her papers.

"Mom," I said, "why don't you wait awhile? Dad will be home soon."

"Soon?" she asked, her voice as puckered as if she'd just sucked lemons. "Eleven-thirty? Midnight?" I guess she heard the sharpness in her words, because she said, "Sorry, Holly. I'm just . . . just tired."

"You used to wait up for him."

"Things used to be different."

"I wish they were the way they used to be."

Mom sighed. "It takes two to make a marriage work."

"Maybe if you . . ."

"That's enough," Mom said firmly. "I don't need a lecture. Please tend to your own business."

Didn't she understand? It *was* my business. I was a part of their marriage.

A flash of car headlights swept against the closed drapes at the den window. Mom gave a start, then without a word left the room and went up the stairs.

Dad came in through the kitchen door. I met him in the kitchen and said, "Hi, Dad. Can I make you a sandwich? Or heat some leftover meat loaf and string beans?"

His glance slipped to the door to the den before it rested on me.

"Mom's gone to bed," I said, "but I'll be glad to cook for you."

"Thanks," Dad said. "How about a meat loaf sandwich? With pickle relish?"

"Sure."

While he hung up his coat and shoulder holster and washed his hands, I put together a dad-size sandwich and poured him a glass of milk.

As he sat at the table and bit into his sandwich, I dropped into the chair opposite his.

"Good sandwich," he managed.

"Dad, could you talk to me?" I asked.

He took another bite and chewed it hungrily before he answered. "About what?"

"About what happened to Cody's parents."

He frowned. "Holly, you know I can't discuss the case with you."

"You don't have to tell me anything you wouldn't tell a reporter," I said. "I'm not asking you to give away secrets. Please, Dad? We'll share information."

"What kind of information have you got?"

What did I have? Nothing. But I couldn't give up. I supposed I could tell Dad about Glenda and her clairvoyant vision. If police used psychics on occasion, they might listen to a clairvoyant too. *Not Dad,* I thought, but I said, "You tell me what you know, and I'll tell you what I find out. If I ask a question that you can answer, fine, but if you can't or don't want to, just say, 'No comment.' "

Dad smiled. " 'No comment'? I'm not a politician."

"Please?"

He demolished half the sandwich, took a long

swig of milk, then said, "Okay. What's your question?"

I rested my arms on the table and leaned forward eagerly. "The man Mr. Arlington saw. Have you found out anything about him? Did you get fingerprints? Anything?"

Dad sighed. He had picked up the other half of his sandwich, but he laid it down. As he looked at me, I could see sorrow well up in his eyes.

"You can't count much on so-called eyewitnesses like Ronald Arlington," Dad said.

"But he saw . . ."

"He *said* he saw. He added that later, not when he was first questioned."

"You're not checking out his story? I don't believe it!"

"Calm down, Holly. You said you wanted to *talk*, not argue."

I fought back my rush of anger. "Sorry," I mumbled.

"We did check out Arlington's story. We have fluorescent powder, special lights, and lenses that can pick up fingerprints on nearly everything," Dad said. "Luis Martinez spent hours going over the grass, the fence, every square inch of the area in which the alleged perp could have been, according to Arlington's description, and he found very little that would support Arlington's story."

"Not even footprints?"

"There were plenty of footprints—by the fence and near the flower bed where the knife was found. They were probably made by Arlington himself in his early morning prowling through the yard. Unfortunately, if there had been any incriminating prints, they'd been obliterated."

"How about on the other side of the fence, where he'd jumped?"

"The ground was hard packed and covered with a thick, uncut mat of St. Augustine grass. Luis found one indentation, which could have been a heel mark, or could have come from any of a number of sources." I had opened my mouth, but before I could speak, Dad anticipated me. "And nothing of any significance was found in the Rollinses' yard."

"Weren't there any fingerprints on the fence?"

"None."

"The murderer could have worn gloves."

"Holly . . ."

"Well, couldn't he?"

"Yes. That would be possible. But wool or fabric gloves would have left small traces."

"What about leather? Leather gloves wouldn't leave traces, would they?" A pain started in my chest and rose into my throat. "And maybe," I said, clinging to hope as if it were a life raft, "Mr. Martinez just didn't look in the right places."

"Not possible. Martinez is thorough." Dad reached across the table and surprised me by clasping my hands. "Holly," he said, "we didn't believe Arlington's story because he added it later— maybe to get some publicity."

"No! He didn't tell you at first because he was afraid the murderer would come back for him!"

Dad continued as though I hadn't said a word. "We thoroughly searched the yard around the back fence. As I told you, we try to find the truth, in spite of the fact that every time there's a murder, a lot of disturbed people confess to the crime, give us false leads, and try to obstruct our investigation.

"Soon after Arlington's story was reported on the TV news, his wife contacted us. She had been at the house late Friday evening. She and Arlington had been going over a list of their possessions, trying to divide them before going into court. She told us that the loud music from the Garnetts' house began to irritate Arlington. He went to the Garnetts' home, and you know what happened after that. At the time he told her nothing about seeing someone jump the fences."

"Just because he didn't tell her—that doesn't mean anything," I countered. "Besides, are you sure she's telling the truth? If she was there, why didn't she come forward and talk to the police too?"

"She said she didn't want to get involved. She also said that Arlington has been getting therapy. He's not only disturbed, he's right on the edge."

I held Dad's hand tightly as tears blurred my vision. "I hoped . . . Oh, Dad, I hoped . . ."

Dad pulled his hand away and busied himself with his sandwich. I knew better than to cry in front of Dad. If I gave in to tears, he'd try to escape, and I wouldn't get to ask him the rest of the questions I had in mind.

I sat up straighter and forced myself to regain control. "Okay, next question," I said. "About

Cody's car." But another thought suddenly hit me, and I gasped.

Dad looked up. "What's the matter?"

"Mr. Arlington," I said. "Maybe he made up that story for a reason. Not because he's a mental and emotional mess but because he's covering up."

Dad nodded. "Same thing occurred to us, that he might have concocted his story to cover up for a crime he had committed himself, but there's nothing that would indicate Arlington had been inside the Garnetts' house."

"Maybe when the murder weapon turns up, you'll discover that his fingerprints are on it."

"That's always a possibility, but I strongly doubt it."

"But it's a possibility! You said so!"

"Holly, don't get your hopes up." Dad polished off the last of his sandwich, finished the milk, and wiped his mouth with the paper napkin I put by his plate. "Any cookies?" he asked.

"Mom bought lots of fruit. There are some really good apples."

"Cookies," Dad said, so I got up and brought him a package of Oreos.

I took one myself, pulled the halves apart, and ate the filling. The tired lines in Dad's face were grooving into each other, and I didn't know how long I could keep him listening, so I spoke quickly, keeping in mind what Sara had said. "Did you get the reports yet from the medical examiner?"

"Yes."

"What was the time of the murder?"

"The estimated time of death was between nine and ten."

"It couldn't be as late as ten, because Mr. Arlington called the police earlier than that."

"He telephoned at nine-thirty-three, to be exact."

"How can you be sure? He said he didn't remember."

"It's recorded on the dispatcher's tape."

"Oh." I should have realized that. "What about the lab? What did they find from the crime scene?"

"We don't have the complete report yet, and I'm not sure how much of it I can repeat to you when we do get it."

"You can tell me if they found something that will help Cody, can't you?"

Dad didn't answer. He squirmed in his chair, and I didn't want to lose him, so I didn't waste time arguing. I said, "Let's go back to my other question. Has the lab checked out Cody's car?"

"From top to bottom."

"And . . . ?"

"I guess I can tell you. They didn't find anything incriminating."

"The sleeping bag was in the trunk. Right?"

"Right."

"And the clothes he drove up there to get?"

"Yes."

"But no bloody clothing?"

"No bloody clothing. Not yet."

"There! You see?" I cried. "The murderer

would have got blood on his clothes. Since Cody didn't, it proves he was telling the truth."

"Not necessarily. The clothes he'd been wearing could be buried anywhere between here and Lake Conroe."

"Dad!" I complained. "Why don't you give up on Cody and look for the real murderer? I know you didn't find enough evidence to prove that Cody was guilty, because you haven't arrested him."

"As of now the evidence we have is circumstantial. We don't arrest anyone unless we have strong, factual proof we can take to the district attorney. In order to get an indictment from the grand jury and a good chance at conviction when the case goes to trial, the DA likes to have an eyewitness to the crime and physical evidence that would place the suspect at the scene without doubt."

I felt an instant rush of hope. "You don't have an eyewitness!"

"Maybe one will still turn up, and—even more likely—maybe we'll get a confession."

"No!" I shouted. "You won't get a confession from Cody, because he didn't do it!"

Dad rolled up the end of the cookie package, pushed back his chair, and got to his feet. "Speaking of Cody," he began, "I'm concerned about you and . . ."

He had a look in his eyes I knew well. "Don't say it, Dad. Please! Cody's suffering terribly because of what happened to his parents, and it's going to get worse because some people will read the newspapers, and watch the television news, and believe he committed the murders. He's being considered guilty until proven innocent, and that's not the way it's supposed to be! It's not fair, Dad."

"I have to think of your safety," he said.

"Cody's not going to hurt me. I promised to help prove he's innocent of the crime, and I have to keep my promise. He's staying with his uncle." I paused. "By this time you've investigated his uncle, haven't you?"

"I have. He seems to be okay. Small businessman. He came into a good-size inheritance, along with Cody's mother, after their mother died six years ago. He invested his share in a restaurant, but it failed. He repaid all his debts—no problem there—and now he owns and manages a shoe store. He's paying on a couple of loans, but nothing he can't handle. He was married once, divorced, no children."

"He's a relative too," I said. "Why isn't he a suspect?"

"No motive," Dad said.

"Where was he at the time the murders took place? Did you ask?"

"Of course I asked."

"Well?"

Dad sighed impatiently and said, "Frank Baker was home watching television. He even told me the plots of the shows he watched."

"Big deal. Anybody could get the plots from reading *TV Guide*."

"Holly," Dad said, "we're getting off the track. Let's get back to what I was trying to say. Until an arrest is made . . ."

I gasped, and Dad amended what he'd said. "*If* and *when* an arrest is made—until then you'll probably be seeing Cody at school, but I don't want you to go out with him."

"How can you be so unfair? You've made up your mind that he's guilty! And other people will too! Think of how people at school might treat him! Cody needs a friend, and I'm his friend."

"Listen to me, Holly," Dad said. "Whether he's guilty or not, I'm making this rule for your protection and my peace of mind."

"But . . ."

"No buts. Bill and I are counting on wrapping up this case within a few days."

I couldn't believe that Dad would do this to me. I was shocked and hurt and angry. My mind kept whirling with thoughts that went nowhere, tripping and splatting over each other, so it wasn't until later, when I was in bed, staring into the darkness, that I remembered I hadn't given Dad my share of the information. It probably didn't mean a thing, but I had the uncomfortable feeling that I should have told him about Glenda Jordan.

Chapter Eight

Sunday. 11:20 A.M. Mom, Dad, and I had been to church. Mom and Dad were smiling and nodding and chatting with people the way a happily married couple is supposed to, I guess. Like the Garnetts' house—proper and lovely on the outside, yet hiding a tragedy no one could see.

I could see.

The thought had jolted me, and I'd pushed it out of my mind. I was letting that weird Glenda Jordan get to me. Both Sunday newspapers had stories about the Garnetts' murders, along with Cody's picture, on the front page. Where he'd been. What he'd said. Sometimes Dad gets mad about information that's leaked from the Homicide Division to the press. It's not supposed to happen, but it does. I ached for Cody. He didn't deserve being tried and convicted by the press.

When the phone rang, I got it. "Uncle Frank

said I could borrow his car," Cody said over the phone. "I thought maybe you'd go for a ride with me."

I took a deep breath. Better to spell it out. "Dad made a rule," I said. "I'm sorry, Cody. I'm terribly sorry, but I can't go out with you."

Cody didn't answer, so I quickly added something of my own to try to make it a little easier for him. "Dad's assigned to the case," I said, "and this is the way it has to be. You know, official rules and all that stuff."

"He's not afraid I'd . . ."

"Of course not! And Dad knows I'm going to help you prove that you're innocent."

Cody sounded incredulous. "You told him you were going to help me, and he doesn't care?"

"He didn't say I couldn't."

"But he won't let you go out with me."

"He just doesn't want us to be alone, but he didn't say you couldn't come over when Mom is here. Why don't you come over and stay for dinner?"

There was a long pause, then Cody asked, "Is your Dad going to be there?"

I heard the back door shut and hopped off my bed to look out the back window. "No. He's leaving now. He probably won't be back until late."

"Okay," Cody said. "I'll see you in about twenty minutes."

I didn't tell Mom my plan, but I trusted her.

Mom's eyelids flipped wide with surprise when she answered the door, but she greeted Cody politely and invited him in. I was proud of Mom. She said all the right things about his parents to comfort him, and she stood aside as I led him to the porch and the glider, which had been set to catch the breeze. At the back of our house is a screened porch. We don't use it much from May through October, when it's hot, but a strong breeze was blowing in from the Gulf; and the porch, decorated with Mom's green-thumb plants, was pleasant.

As Cody sat down, the glider gently rocking on its stand, he glanced at the notepad and pen on the low table nearby and asked, "What's that for?"

"We need to write down everything we can think of to help us solve this case."

Cody sighed. The color had returned to his face, and he had lost the tired-old-man slouch, but his eyes showed his sorrow. "I don't want to talk about it or think about it. It's all a nightmare, Holly. I close my eyes, and all I can see is blood."

Shocked, I blurted out, "They let you see the murder scene?"

"No!" Cody answered. His eyes widened with fear. "Look . . . what I said didn't come out right. I wasn't there when it happened. And I wasn't there later. I know that my parents were stabbed, so it doesn't take much imagination to figure out there must have been a lot of blood. You understand what I meant, don't you, Holly?"

I shivered, not sure I really did understand, but I answered, "Yes. I'm sorry, Cody."

He leaned against the back of the glider and closed his eyes. Finally he opened them and asked, "Do you know what I'd like to be doing right now?

I'd like to say, 'Grab your bathing suit, and let's drive down to Galveston.' I'd like to tell you crazy jokes and laugh with you. I'd like to hold you and kiss you. But I've got this terrible monster on my back and it won't go away." He sighed. "Will it ever?"

"When the investigation is over and the murderer is caught, the monster *will* go away."

"I don't know that it will. I'm the only suspect."

"Not really. There's Mr. Arlington."

Cody shook his head. "He didn't do it, Holly. He's having trouble with reality. Uncle Frank was over at the house this morning to pick up some of my clothes and other stuff I needed. One of the neighbors told him that Mr. Arlington's wife and his therapist signed him into a clinic for treatment."

"I'm not about to give up on Mr. Arlington as a suspect. He has real problems. What if he turned violent because the music in your house was too loud?" A thought struck me. "Cody," I asked, "why was the music too loud?"

He stared at me. "What do you mean?"

"Your neighbors said you kept the volume up when you played your tapes and CDs or the radio, but on Friday night you weren't there. Your parents wouldn't play music that loud, would they?"

"No," Cody said, an expression of wonder in his face. "Of course they wouldn't."

"Did you leave the radio on when you left your house around seven-thirty?"

"No. I hadn't turned it on."

"Was music playing when you came back to get the key or when you left?"

"No."

"Then who turned it on?"

"Whoever murdered my parents? But why?" He looked down at his hands in anguish. "Oh, Holly, what if someone was trying to make it look like I did it?"

"It's possible." I could think of another reason —to drown out any shouts or cries for help—but I wasn't about to tell Cody that and add to his nightmares.

"When you left the house the last time, did you lock the door behind you?"

"I didn't have to. Both front and back doors lock automatically. Why'd you ask?"

"Because the police found no sign of forced entry. Either someone had a key, or your parents knew them and let them in."

Cody groaned. "That's what your father and his partner told me over and over again. They kept saying that I had a key. The only key."

"No one else had a key? A cleaning woman? Your uncle?"

"I don't think so. Dad was uptight about security."

"Then forget about keys, and try to remember who your parents might have invited into their home. Did they have any enemies?"

Cody looked up. "I don't know. If my dad had enemies, they could only have been people involved in some of his business deals. Dad had a short fuse. Sometimes I'd hear him on the phone yelling at someone. He wasn't nice about it."

Although I'd read about drivers so stupid that they'd shoot at another driver who'd cut in front of them, I couldn't imagine that people in business would murder someone just because he was rude and yelled at them.

"What kind of business was your father in?" I asked.

"All sorts of stuff," Cody said. "He invested in different kinds of businesses. Sometimes he made a lot of money. Sometimes he didn't."

"Did he talk about these business deals?"

"Not to me, he didn't, but Mom knew about them and wasn't too happy about some of them. A couple of times lately I walked in while they were arguing, but they always shut up tight when I was around."

"Tell me what they said."

"I don't know. I only caught a few words. *Risky*, that was one of them. Mom used that a couple of times lately. She was upset about something Dad was doing, but I don't know what. I honestly didn't pay much attention."

"Did your uncle Frank get into any business deals with your father?"

"Uncle Frank?" Cody looked at me in amazement. "Uncle Frank didn't want any part of Dad's business operations. In fact, he had a lot to say against a couple of them. Mom said Frank shouldn't butt in, and Dad yelled at Mom for having told Frank about them. Dad hated it when

Frank tried to tell him anything about business. I remember he yelled that Frank shouldn't have the nerve to tell anyone anything about how to run a business, seeing that Frank could barely keep his head above water."

"If he knew he'd get yelled at, then Frank must have thought what he had to say about your father's business was too important to ignore. What did Frank say about the deals? Can you remember?"

"Stuff like, 'That's not too bright,' " Cody said. " 'Shady. Much too risky.' " His eyes widened. "Maybe that's the same deal Mom was complaining about. She used the word *risky*."

I began to get excited. "Cody, Dad said there was a computer in your father's office at home. Did he keep any business records on this computer?"

Cody sat up a little straighter. "He could have. When he was home, he spent a lot of time in his office."

"Could we check it out?"

Cody winced. "I—I don't want to ever go back inside the house again."

"I'll go if you'll give me your key."

"I don't have it. I think the police do." He thought a moment. "There is an extra key, come to think of it. After Mom locked herself out of the house a couple of times, she hid one inside a Coke can on a shelf in the garage." He frowned. "I forgot about it. I didn't tell your dad."

"Listen," I said. "Have I got your permission?"

"I don't know," Cody replied. "I don't think you should be in the house, Holly."

I sank back against the cushions, suddenly visualizing the living room the way Cody had and wishing I hadn't made the offer, but I'd discovered something that should be investigated. I had to follow the lead to prove to Dad that Cody was innocent. I needed to do it for Cody's sake and for mine. "Is there a way to your father's office without having to go through the living room?"

"Yes, but wait a few days," Cody said, "and I'll . . . I'll try to go with you—if it's okay with your Dad, that is. The police are through with the crime scene, so they gave permission to have the house cleaned. Uncle Frank made arrangements with somebody to show up there on Thursday to scrub the walls and take away the carpeting in the living room. Frank's going to put the house on the market for me."

"Is Frank your guardian?"

"He is now. And he's the executor of my parents' wills. Mr. Ormond is doing all the legal stuff for us. I asked Frank to help me out by taking care of all the business matters. He said he would. He's been real good about everything."

"Thursday is four days from now." I thought about Dad saying he and Bill hoped to wrap up the case soon, and I began to get frantic. "I want to look at those records as soon as possible, and I'd rather go by myself."

Cody looked at me oddly. "In spite of what . . . what happened in the house?"

"I'm not going to feel very comfortable about it, but it has to be done," I said. "Maybe I won't go alone. I'll ask Sara if she'll come with me."

As Cody hesitated, I lightly touched his arm. A muscle twitched, and he jumped.

"You can't go in there, Cody. You shouldn't go. But listen to me. I have to find out, as fast as I can, as much as I can about who might have murdered your parents."

"Maybe you shouldn't," he murmured so softly I could scarcely hear him.

Startled, I repeated, "Shouldn't find out?"

"No. I meant go inside the house."

"You can give me permission." When Cody didn't answer, I persisted. "It's your house. You'll inherit everything from your parents, won't you?"

"Yes," Cody said. "I'm the only beneficiary." He jumped to his feet and paced around the small porch like a lion trapped inside a small cage. "It makes everything worse, doesn't it? The police will think that . . ."

"Cody!" I stepped in front of him and grabbed his shoulders. "I told you I believe in you, and I'm going to do everything I can to help you. But I have to do it soon. Trust me. We both know you're innocent. Right?"

His voice was firm as he looked into my eyes. "Right, Holly. Absolutely."

"Okay then?"

"The key's on the third shelf, just behind the side door into the garage," he told me. "It will open the dead bolts on both the front and back door." His glance shifted toward the kitchen. "What's your dad going to say about this?"

"You told me the police were through with the crime scene. If I want to go inside the house, I

104

can, without answering to anyone except the owner—and that's you."

A brief smile flicked across Cody's lips. "You're stubborn, Holly. I didn't know how stubborn. Does it go with the red hair?"

I took both of his hands in mine and tried to match his smile. "I'm not stubborn. I'm . . . intent. That's it . . . *intent.* I'm intent on discovering who committed the crime."

I leaned forward and lightly kissed Cody's lips.

For an instant he trembled. Then he wrapped his arms around me, and his mouth pressed hard against mine.

Just as suddenly he pulled away, burying his head against my shoulder. "Not now," he mumbled.

I held him tightly, giving him time to get himself in hand. *Time,* I thought. *We haven't much time.* But I willed myself to be still, to stay calm.

In a few minutes Cody stood back and brushed some tendrils of my hair away from my cheek. His voice broke as he said, "The medical examiner released my parents' bodies to a funeral home. The funeral will be Tuesday afternoon at four o'clock. Will you come?"

"Of course," I said.

By the time Mom called us to dinner, my thoughts had jumped to a movie I'd seen. A police detective went to the murder victim's funeral because he was sure the murderer would be there. I was thinking like Sara now. Or maybe like a detective. Some of those TV cops were pretty clever.

It stood to reason that many of Mr. Garnett's business associates would show up for the funeral. If I could access his computer records, I might be able to match names to faces and point out possible suspects to Dad.

It might work. It was the only thing I could think of to do.

Mom had a lot to say to me after Cody left that evening. When she finally stopped, I told her, "Dad just said I couldn't go out with Cody. He didn't say Cody couldn't come here."

"You know good and well what your father meant."

"Mom!" I wailed. "You think Cody's guilty! Dad thinks he's guilty! Everybody at school's going to think so too! No one's giving Cody a chance! How would you feel if a terrible crime was committed and everyone took it for granted that *you* did it? Cody lost both of his parents, and now he's under this awful suspicion."

Mom gave a miserable sigh, then walked over and put her arms around me. "The world's full of hurts," she murmured against my hair. "I'm sorry that Cody is having to experience so many of them while he's so young."

"We have to help Cody, Mom," I said.

I could feel Mom's muscles tense. Then she shivered as she stepped back and faced me. "*You're* our prime concern, Holly. I wouldn't know how I'd exist without you. Regardless of how you feel about helping Cody, I go along with your father. Please don't invite Cody back to the house. We can't allow you to see him."

*   *   *

Monday. 8:30 A.M. Cody didn't show up at school.

It was just as well, because Monday was one of the worst days I ever had to live through. It would have been a lot tougher for him.

Bellaire High has a large student body, and I'm sure that every last person, even if they had never heard about Cody and me before Friday, knew about us now. As I walked to first-period English lit., kids in the hall would stop talking and stare at me. Some of those I knew would pat my shoulder or touch my arm and murmur things like, "Oh, Holly, weren't you scared?"

"He didn't do it," I told them.

"Holly, how awful! You were dating him!"

"Cody always seemed so nice. None of us knew what he was really like."

"He didn't do it," I answered.

I saw two of Cody's friends standing by their lockers, and I hoped they'd come to his defense, but they quickly looked away as we made eye contact and hurried down the hall.

"I'm so sorry, Holly," the voices went on.

"Just be thankful you weren't there!"

"I'm glad nothing terrible happened to *you*."

"He didn't do it," I said to each of them through a smothering haze. "He didn't do it!" I practically shouted.

Then Sara shoved her way toward me, put an arm around my shoulders, and walked me the rest of the way to class. "Don't get mad at them," she

107

said. "They don't know." She smiled and gave my shoulder a squeeze. "We're going to show them. Right?"

I took a long breath and felt the bubbling boil inside me melt down to a simmer. "Right," I said.

As we settled into our seats opposite each other in lit., I leaned toward Sara and said quietly, "Have you got your family's Jeep today?" I live just a few blocks from school and usually walk the distance, but Sara lives farther away. Either her father drops her off and her mother picks her up, or she gets to drive the family's old Jeep.

Sara nodded. "Need a lift home?"

"Do you have time to take me to the Garnetts' house?"

Her mouth fell open, and before she found words to fill it, I quickly outlined the plan.

The moment I'd finished, she asked, "What good will it do to look through Mr. Garnett's computer? What do you hope to find?"

"I'm not sure," I said. "But maybe there'll be enough about his business deals to give us an idea if one of them isn't as legal at it should have been."

"Can't you ask your dad to do this?"

"Sara," I said, "Dad is so sure that Cody is guilty, he'd probably insist that checking out Mr. Garnett's computer records would be a big waste of time and wouldn't lead anywhere."

Sara pursed her lips as she thought. I told her about the movie that showed a detective attending a funeral, and that caught her attention. "I saw that," she said, "and the funeral scene in the rain was really creepy. But we'd have to know who was who to make it work."

"We could listen in. We could ask questions."

"Spy?"

"Whatever you want to call it."

She thought a moment. "Do you want to go to the house right after school?"

"If that's okay with you."

"I guess so. Okay," she said.

The bell rang, and we got down to business. I have no idea what we studied during lit. or during the rest of the day. All I could think about was what I hoped to accomplish.

Monday. 2:55 P.M. When Sara parked the Jeep in front of the Garnetts' house, the street was empty. The "large lovelies" stood proudly and silently apart. Glenda Jordan's house retreated under its umbrella of leafy green. And the Arlington house squatted with shades covering its glass eyes, so withdrawn that it ignored the yellowed newspapers that lay on the walk and against the front door.

Sara stared at the ornate lead glass in the Garnetts' front door. "Are you really sure you want us to go in there?" she murmured.

"Yes," I answered.

"I feel like this isn't real, that we're on a TV show."

"It's not TV. It's real. Sara, we've got to do it for the sake of justice."

Sara didn't move. "Don't you feel it?" she whispered.

"Feel what?"

"The staring, Holly. I know it's weird, but I feel like somebody is staring at us."

Chapter Nine

I'm the one who's supposed to be supersensitive to things, according to that clairvoyant neighbor I told you about," I said, glad that Sara didn't know how hard I was working to keep my voice steady. "You've just seen too many movies. Come on. If the key's where Cody said it would be, we'll go in the back door."

Reluctantly, Sara followed me to the garage. The Coke can was in place, and the key dropped into my hand.

The dead bolt lock on the back door must have been kept oiled, because it slid open smoothly. The door opened without a sound, and I stepped into the kitchen. Without thinking, I automatically tucked the key into my pocket.

Even though the air conditioners had been kept running, the house smelled musty and stale, with the tang of a pine-scented cleaner around the edges. Somebody—probably Frank—must have already tried to clean up the living room. My imagination went into high speed, and I had to take a deep breath to keep from gagging. I waited for Sara to join me, then shut the door firmly. The dead bolt slid into place.

"It's awfully quiet in here," Sara whispered.

"We don't have to whisper," I told her. I spoke normally, but my voice banged against my ears and bounced off the white-enameled kitchen cabinets, smudged now with fingerprint powder. "Come on. Cody said to follow the hall that leads from the den. His dad's office is the first room on the left."

"The den? It's not . . . ?"

"No. They were murdered in the living room."

We stepped silently through the den, then entered the hallway.

"Should we turn on lights?" Holly whispered.

"No. It's daylight. We don't need lights."

"But all the drapes are closed. It's so dim in here."

The door to the office, which faced the front street, was open. It wasn't a large room, and file cabinets against one wall made it even smaller. A computer sat squarely in the middle of a bulky, cherry-wood desk, its printer off to one side.

"I'm going to open the drapes," Sara said and reached for the cord. As sunlight streamed in and the room brightened, she gave a sigh of relief. "Okay," she said. "What next?"

I turned on the computer and waited until it

came up with a menu. Sara leaned over my shoulder, watching. I hadn't worked with this brand of computer before, but it wasn't long before I had the feel of it and had reached Mr. Garnett's list of documents.

The names of the documents made no sense, so I jotted them down on a nearby notepad. "We'll have to try them, one at a time, until we reach whatever we're looking for."

"Maybe we won't find what you want," Sara said. "Whatever's on his computer isn't secret. There was no special access code. If he was into something illegal, he wouldn't have it in plain view for anyone who looked into his computer, would he?"

"I don't know. There's no modem, so this computer isn't hooked into his computer downtown or any system where someone might be able to access his computer. He probably thought anything in this computer would be for his eyes only."

"Okay. Try the first one," Sara said. "I don't want to be here any longer than we have to."

When the first document came up on the screen, Sara whistled. "Wow! I knew the Garnetts had money, but . . ."

I quickly pressed SAVE and EXIT as my face grew hot with embarrassment. "We have no business looking at his income tax records."

"We won't tell what we saw," Sara said. "Hurry up. Try the next document."

A string of French names and numbers came up.

"What in the world is that?" Sara asked.

I caught a few words straight out of California. "It's a wine list," I told her. "There must be a wall of wine racks somewhere in the house to hold all these bottles."

We skimmed as fast as we could, trying not to be nosy, through a list of insurance records that covered life, medical, house, cars, and jewelry. Sara grabbed my hand as we came to a listing of jewelry that was insured. "Wait! Look at that! What must it be like to wear a necklace that's insured for twenty-five thousand dollars? Was that stolen?"

"I don't think so. I think the murderer stole only the jewelry she was wearing." I tried to remember what the newspaper had reported: Mrs. Garnett's engagement and wedding rings, a watch, and a narrow gold bracelet.

Discouraged at my lack of success in finding anything about Mr. Garnett's business dealings, I entered the next document and almost exited it before I realized what I had found. Leaning forward, I said, "Sara, here's a list of property Mr. Garnett owns—some of it with other people."

Sara leaned forward too and pointed at the screen. "There's their lake house," she said. "Still under mortgage. This house too."

"Look at this entry," I said. "It's a warehouse, and he didn't own it by himself. There's a co-owner. I'm going to print out the information."

"There's nothing wrong with owning a warehouse," Sara said.

"I know, but maybe there's something in one of

these documents that tells what's kept in the warehouses."

"Then you'd better keep looking," Sara said.

The house was silent except for the low hum of the printer and the rustle of paper as it slid into the tray.

Sara suddenly grabbed my shoulder so hard that it hurt. "Did you hear that?" she asked.

"Hear what?" I'd been concentrating so hard on what was being printed that I hadn't been paying attention, but as I listened intently, my memory brought back the tiniest of clicks.

Nervously I pushed back my chair and tiptoed to the door to the hallway, Sara close behind me.

For a moment we were silent, except for our rapid breathing, and I shook my head at her. "Hello!" I called out. "Is anyone here?"

The air-conditioning unit for the downstairs cycled on. "Houses just make noise. You didn't hear anything."

"Yes I did."

"Then it must have been a sound from outside."

Sara shook her head. "No. It came from inside the house."

"Do you hear anything now?"

"No."

"Come on," I told her. "Let's bring up those other documents and see if there's anything on them that will help."

As I sat before the computer again, Sara said, "I wish you could see your barrette. The amber is glowing."

I gasped and clapped a hand to the top of my head, my fingers tingling as I touched the warm stone.

"What did I say?" Sara asked. "Why do you look so scared? You're sitting in the sun, and it's highlighting the amber in your barrette. Is there anything wrong with that?"

"Th-The amber . . . ," I stammered. "I-It's . . ." The words that would explain jammed in my throat, choking me. I forced myself to regain control and said, "I'll tell you all about it later, Sara. Right now we've got work to do."

The next document I brought up was a list of stocks, bonds, and other investments. I quickly scrolled through that and went into the last document, which was a detailed accounting of bank transactions throughout the current year, with notations—most in abbreviations—that seemed to indicate the sources of the income.

"Wow!" I said when I saw the business the warehouse had generated. There were pages and pages in this document, but I went into PRINT and the copy began sliding into the tray.

"This may be important," I murmured, but as Sara hung over my shoulder, reading the entries I'd pulled from the tray, I felt prickly, as if someone were watching me, and my gaze was drawn to the doorway.

I froze, too frightened to scream, as I looked into Glenda Jordan's dark, compelling eyes. She held a finger to her lips, and I heard the words in my mind: *Be very, very quiet.*

I was so frightened I could hear my heart

pounding. I reached up and pulled Sara's head down to my shoulder. Whispering into her ear, I said, "Everything's okay. Whatever you do, don't scream. Don't even make a sound."

"Wha—?" Sara began, but I clapped a hand over her mouth.

I stood, releasing Sara. The printer had finished, so I turned off the computer and snatched the finished pages.

Sara saw Glenda and grabbed my arm in terror, but I shook my head, held a finger to my own lips, and quietly walked to meet Glenda, dragging Sara with me.

As we drew near, Glenda stepped just inside the room and whispered, "Someone evil is hiding in this house. You must leave. Now."

Somehow we managed to walk down the hall and through the den and kitchen behind Glenda, but my legs wobbled so badly it was hard to stay upright. I fought back the panic that made me want to break free and run. I could feel eyes on my back, and I jumped at the sounds of our own footsteps. What if this person who was hiding suddenly leaped out at us? What if he ran down the hall after us? Where was he? What was he planning to do?

Sara smothered a whimper, and I clutched her hand tightly. We reached the back door, burst through, and raced down the driveway toward the Jeep.

Leaning against it, sucking in air with loud, noisy gasps, we waited for Glenda, who approached us calmly. The air was still and heavy with heat. All I could hear was the excited yapping of the Rollinses' dog, Tiger, in the yard on the next street and the loud cawing of two grackles in a nearby tree.

"You called me, and I came," Glenda said, looking at me.

"I didn't call you," I insisted. "Sara and I were working on the computer."

"I know," Glenda said. "I saw you, in my mind, so I entered the house."

Sara looked from Glenda to me and back to Glenda. "We made sure the door was locked with a dead bolt," Sara said. "How did you get in?"

"The door was ajar."

"No. We locked it," I insisted, before I realized what she had said. "Then someone opened it." I glanced toward the house. "Who? Who's in there?"

"I don't know," Glenda answered.

"You didn't see him?"

"I saw you . . . and your friend."

With a jolt I realized that the person in the house could be the murderer I was trying so hard to find. "S-Sara and I can w-watch both the front and back doors and make sure whoever's in there doesn't leave. Glenda, why don't you run home and call the police?"

"It would do no good to call the police," Glenda answered. "The one who was in the house with you left soon after we did."

"How? We would have seen him," Sara said.

I realized the Rollinses' dog barking frenzy

meant just one thing. "Whoever it was went over the back fence, didn't he?" I asked.

"I have no idea," Glenda said. "My thoughts were tuned to yours alone. I could sense the evil that was threatening you and came to lead you from the house. For the moment that's all that matters."

"Glenda," I said, "if there was someone in the house who wanted to harm us, then *you* could have been in danger."

"Whether or not there was danger, I can't be sure. But with the strong evil that chose to conceal itself near you, I felt the risk was too strong to ignore."

"Thank you for coming," I murmured.

Sara looked at me oddly but she said, "Yes, thanks."

"You're welcome. Sara, is it?"

"Oh, I'm sorry. I didn't introduce you," I said, embarrassed. "Glenda Jordan, this is Sara Madison."

Glenda and Sara nodded politely to each other. Then Glenda turned to me. "I've been expecting you."

"Uh . . . well, I . . ."

"Together we may discover the identity of the murderer, amber girl."

"Amber girl?" Sara murmured.

"I . . . uh . . . I don't want to re-create the murder scene," I blurted out. "I don't want to see it!"

Glenda laid her cool fingertips on my arm. "I

must not have explained well," she said. "We couldn't possibly re-create the actions that took place at the time of the murder. Clairvoyants work with visions of what is happening at the moment."

"Then what would you . . . ?"

"What we would attempt to do is offer a receptive climate in which the Garnetts could respond, possibly leading us to the name of their murderer."

"I don't get it," Sara said.

But I did. Leaning against the side of the Jeep for support, I managed to mutter, "You're t-talking about seeking their spirits and bringing them back, aren't you?"

"Spirits?" Sara repeated.

"It's not a question of bringing them back," Glenda explained. "In acts of sudden violence, spirits cling to their surroundings, hoping for the justice that will mean their release."

Sara moved closer to me and tugged on my arm. "We've got to leave now, Holly," she said. "If I don't come home soon, Mom will start worrying about me."

"Okay," I answered quickly. I was just as eager as Sara to leave this woman and her invitation to call up spirits. I scrambled to climb into the passenger side of the Jeep and managed to thank Glenda again.

"Just call me when you are ready," Glenda said. "But don't wait too much longer."

Sara took off too fast, and I was glad we were wearing our seat belts. "Slow down," I insisted.

"You slow down too," she said, and as we reached the corner, she eased up on the gas pedal.

"What are you talking about?"

"I saw your face when you were talking to Glenda. You were seriously thinking about doing what she wants you to do, weren't you?"

"No!" I said. "Well, maybe, but just *maybe*. What if she can find out the name of the murderer? I want to help Cody, don't I?"

"Not by fooling around with weird people who claim to seek spirits. Look at all that scary stuff she put us through. Maybe she wants some publicity. Maybe she's just plain nuts. What did she mean by calling you 'amber girl'?"

"It's because of my barrette. She told me that amber has mystical powers, that people don't choose amber. It chooses them."

"Booga-booga, hocus-pocus!" Sara threw me a disgusted glance.

"Just suppose she saved our lives. The door was open, and she came to warn us."

"Come on, Holly. I bet she opened it herself. If one extra key was hidden, there may have been more. People keep extra keys hidden around their property. She probably found a key and used it."

"I don't think there's more than one extra key kept around the house," I said, suddenly remembering I hadn't returned the key to its hiding place. "Cody knew of only one key. Remember, Glenda said she saw us *inside* the house, felt the evil, and came."

"Big nothing. Be reasonable. Think like a TV detective."

"A TV detective?"

"Sure. Here's what the detective would say: If

Glenda looked out her window, she could have seen a strange car parked in front of the house. She could have seen that the drapes to Mr. Garnett's office were suddenly open, so she figured someone was in the house. Then, if she looked in the window, she could have seen us."

"There's more to it than that, Sara. Honestly. I got her mental message. I looked up and saw Glenda in the doorway. Then into my mind came the thought that we should be very quiet. I *felt* the danger."

"She's into mental telepathy too?" Sara sounded angry. "And you're buying that stuff? Come on, Holly. What's happening to you?"

I didn't answer. I couldn't. And Sara was quiet. We were almost into Bellaire when she added more gently, "Holly, the house is scary because we know what happened there, so I can see why you'd start believing the weird things that woman said. But think about it. You said you don't believe she opened the door herself, that someone else did."

"That's right," I said. "That noise you thought you heard . . . that could have been the back door opening or shutting."

"Okay, let's say that's what I heard, and someone else opened the door, not Glenda. Now hear me out. I hate to do this, but who'd be the best one to know where extra keys to the house are hidden?"

I twisted toward her as the answer shocked me.

"And who knew you'd be in the house?"

"Sara, don't say it. Don't even think it!" I cried.

"You'd better think about it," Sara answered. "No matter how much you want to believe in him, you've got to face the truth. Who else could have come in the house so easily and at just the time we'd be there? Only one person—Cody."

Chapter Ten

Monday. 4:35 P.M. When we arrived at my house, Sara came in to say hello to Mom, but we found a note she'd left saying she had to stay for parent meetings. There was frozen lasagna to microwave.

"Come on home with me," Sara suggested. "This morning Mom started a pot of beef stew to slow-cook all day while she was at work. There's going to be plenty, and I think you need some company."

Mrs. Madison was a great cook, and I could almost taste her stew. The dinner would be noisy and fun, and for just a moment I was jealous that Sara had that kind of family and I didn't. Ashamed of myself, I started to turn down her invitation, but I didn't want to eat alone. I thanked her for the invitation, the ride, and everything and said I'd come.

Sara wandered into the screened porch. "Your mom has a real green thumb," she said. There was silence for a moment; then she said, "What's this?"

As I joined her, I saw that she was holding the pad of paper I'd put on the table when I'd thought that Cody and I could try to figure things out.

"What does this mean—'*Pros* and *Cons*'?" Sara asked.

"Oh, that," I said. "Nothing. Cody and I were going to work on it, but we didn't." I reached for the pad, but she pulled it away.

"Pros and cons," she said and sat on the glider. "Writing them down is a good idea."

"Not now."

"Yes, now," Sara said. "It might help you see how everything fits. Come on, Holly. I did what you wanted me to do, so now sit down and let's figure this out."

Unwillingly, I perched beside her. Sara had picked up the pen and was already writing. I didn't say anything, but I could see she had written only on the *Cons* side of the page.

"This isn't going to help," I said.

"Yes it is. I'll read these aloud, one by one. You come up with the *Pros*. Okay, let's start. Cody returned to the house to get the key to the lake house. He was there during the time the medical examiner said the murders took place."

"The medical examiner adds extra time before and after, depending on the temperature of the room and so on. He can't be exact on the time down to the minute. Cody left *before* his parents

125

were killed. And there's something important the media left out. The radio wasn't on while Cody was there. Somebody turned it on later."

"Can anyone help him prove this? How about the neighbor across the street who saw him drive away?"

"No." I could feel my temper rising. "She couldn't remember when she heard the music, but it's true. Cody said so."

"Don't get defensive," Sara said quietly. "Let's stick to the facts and keep our minds open, and we may figure out something that will help Cody."

That made sense. I took a couple of deep breaths and forced myself to calm down.

"Next point," Sara continued. "There's nothing to prove that Cody was ever at the lake house."

"He stopped on the way back for something to eat."

"Good," she said, her pen poised over the *Pro* side. "Did anybody identify him?"

Miserable, I shook my head. "He stopped at one of those little doughnut shops off the road. He didn't remember which one."

"Let's hope that the police checked them all. Ask your dad." She studied the list. "There was no sign of forced entry, and Cody had a key to the house."

"Sara! A lot of the time when there's a crime, the police say there was no sign of forced entry. That's because most people open their door if someone rings the bell."

"I'll give him that," she said, and wrote on the *Pro* side.

"Don't forget to put down on the *Pro* side that there was a robbery," I said. Rings and watches and a gold bracelet." I didn't tell her Dad's opinion that the robbery could have been faked in order to lead investigators in the wrong direction.

When Sara had finished writing, she asked, "Anything else?"

"Yes. Cody's car checked out clean."

As Sara wrote, the world became a little brighter. The *Pro* column was growing longer than the *Con* side.

"Does Cody get all his parents' money?" Sara asked.

"What does that have to do with anything?"

"A lot," she said. "It gives him a motive."

I didn't answer, but she wrote in the *Con* column anyway. "Anything else?" she asked.

I shook my head and got to my feet. "You were wrong. Writing everything down didn't help. At least the *Pro* column is as long as the *Con*."

As Sara stood, she dropped the pad and pen on the table. "It doesn't matter how long the lists are, Holly. What matters is what's in them. Cody could have been on the scene at the time of the murders, he has no one to back up his alibi, and he had a motive."

My head began to hurt, and I felt sick to my stomach. "He didn't do it," I insisted.

"I'm just saying he could have." Sara grabbed my shoulders and forced me to look at her. "Holly, don't be so stubborn about this that you do something crazy. What if Cody did commit the murders and you keep seeing him?"

"Sara, I can't believe that Cody's the killer. That would be giving up, and I can't do that. I promised to help him."

"You're not listening. You're not even trying to have an open mind."

Angrily, I jerked away from her. "What if *you* were the one suspected of murdering someone? Wouldn't you want me to stick by you? Wouldn't you expect me to keep believing in you?"

"That's different."

"How?"

"Because I wouldn't murder anyone."

"Neither would Cody!"

"How much do you really know about him?" Sara scooped up the pad of paper and shoved it at me. "Read this. Think about it."

I knocked the pad out of her hand. "Stop it!" I shouted and began to cry.

Sara walked into the kitchen. I could hear her filling a glass with cold water from the spigot in the refrigerator door. She returned and handed me the water. "Here," she said. "This might help."

I wiped my face with a ragged tissue I found in my pocket and gulped some of the water.

"Wash your face," Sara said, trying to make her voice cheerful, "and we'll head for my house and Mom's beef stew."

I put down the glass of water and stood up,

shaking my head. "Thanks, but I'm going to stay here," I said.

"Please come, Holly."

"No. I'm not hungry, and I feel like being alone."

"I didn't mean to upset you. I just wanted to make you see both sides of the situation."

"You don't understand," I told Sara. "Can you think of anything worse than being tried and convicted for a murder you didn't commit—especially the murder of your own parents? It's horrible enough to lose your parents." My voice was rising and my breathing was becoming raspy, so I forced myself to calm down before I said, "I promised Cody I'd help him prove his innocence. I have to. I can't let an injustice pass. It would haunt me forever."

"You don't have to keep that promise. Not if . . ."

"Sara, do you remember before we were friends when I was in Ms. Donavan's sixth grade? There was a girl named Paula. Mindy was in that class too."

Sara made a face as she thought. "I don't remember a Paula, but Mindy? What does this have to do with them? You're not friends with Mindy, and neither am I."

My cheeks burned, and I could hardly look at Sara as I answered. "On Ms. Donavan's desk was a little Lladro statue of a girl reading. Well, Mindy was playing with it. I remember so clearly. Paula told her not to. Then Mindy got mad, because she always wanted to be boss, and tossed it to Paula. Paula missed catching it, and it broke. When Ms. Donavan saw it, she looked heartbroken. I let Paula take the blame."

"So?"

"You don't understand, Sara. I saw what happened and didn't tell Ms. Donavan the truth."

Sara stared at me for a minute, then said, "Good gosh, Holly, that was in sixth grade! And if Paula dropped it, she did break it, didn't she?"

"Technically, but . . ."

"What are you telling me? That you're on some kind of guilt trip? That you're being so stubborn about Cody's innocence because of something that happened way back when you were twelve?"

"Sara!" I repeated, as I felt the tears start again. "You don't understand."

"You're right. I'm trying, but I don't."

"Then go home! Please go home!"

Sara looked at me. I could see she was hurt, but I didn't even walk to the door with her.

In all my life I had never felt so miserable. I wanted to call after Sara and beg her to come back. I needed a friend like Sara. I remembered when we'd started spending more and more time together. I always liked the noisy Madisons, and when my parents' marriage started to fall apart, I'd wanted Mom to turn into warm, funny Mrs. Madison. For a long, selfish moment I wished I could run far away from Cody and his horrendous problems.

I put my hands over my face and sobbed loudly,

the way a little child would cry. What did it matter? There was no one to hear me. I was alone.

Monday. *8:40 P.M.* By the time Mom arrived, I had pulled myself together. I greeted her by throwing my arms around her neck and hugging her tightly. "I missed you," I told her. "I love you, Mom."

"My goodness!" Mom answered. She hugged me back, and it felt so good I hung on for a while.

Finally, as I stepped back, Mom studied my face and quietly asked, "Want to talk about it, Holly? Can I help?"

I tried to hang on to a smile and said, "I just needed a hug. And to tell you I love you. I guess I need to hear it too."

"Oh, sweetie, you know I love you."

"You haven't called me sweetie since I was a little girl." I chuckled.

Mom laughed too. "I haven't because you strongly insisted you were much too old to be called sweetie."

"I know," I said, "but this time it sounded good." I followed Mom to her bedroom and flopped on the end of her bed while she changed clothes. "You used to call Dad sweetie too. I never heard him complain."

As she backed out of the closet, Mom gave me a sharp look. "That's enough about your father and me."

I didn't want to break the warm rapport between us, so I quickly changed the subject. "It was awful at school today, Mom. Everybody stared at me as if I were lucky to still be alive, and some of them said things like . . . Well, I guess a few of them were trying to be nice, but some were just . . ."

I rolled onto my back. "You know those fish in the aquarium who come right up to the glass and stare at you with those goggle eyes, while their mouths are going back and forth and back and forth? Well, that's how I felt—like I was getting stared at by hundreds of those nosy fish."

Mom sat down beside me. As she finished buttoning the last button on her blouse, she took my hand and held it tightly. She didn't say anything. She didn't need to. I relaxed. Suddenly I felt as if things would work out. I'd find the answers that would help Cody, and soon everything would be all right.

The phone rang, and I answered. Cody's voice was low and dry. "About the funeral tomorrow . . . ," he began.

"I'll be there," I assured him.

"No," he said. "You can't. That is, it's going to be a private ceremony tomorrow morning with just Uncle Frank and me there." His voice dropped so I could hardly hear. "My parents are going to be cremated."

"Oh," I murmured, and I couldn't think of a thing to say.

Cody broke the silence. "I don't like it either," he said, "but Mr. Ormond—you know, my attorney—said it would be better. With any other kind of funeral service, the place would be overrun with cameramen and reporters."

His voice broke in a sob, and I hurried to cover for him. "I'm sorry, Cody. I can't even begin to guess how hard this is for you."

"It's awful," he said. "It tore me up to lose both of my parents, but now . . . well, it's like I can't give them the respect they deserve. I don't think they would have wanted—I mean, I think they'd have preferred a proper burial."

"I'm sorry," I said. "Oh, Cody, I'm so very, very sorry."

"Holly," Cody said, and I could hear a subtle change in his voice, "you promised to help me, and I'm counting on you. Mr. Ormond was talking to your dad, and . . . uh . . . well, all I'm asking is, since *you* know I'm not the killer, could you . . . uh . . . put in a good word for me with him?"

My stomach clutched. Cody expected me to influence Dad? Cody didn't know what he was asking. "It will take more than that. It will take proof," I answered.

"Right," Cody said, as though he hadn't heard me or didn't understand. He simply repeated, "Holly, I'm counting on you."

Dad actually got home before Mom went to bed. He sank into his favorite comfortable chair and leaned his head back against the headrest. He smothered a belch and pressed one hand against his chest. "One of these days I'm going to wind things up early, and I'll make it home in time to enjoy a real dinner," he said.

Mom got a cynical look on her face. She opened her mouth to answer, then quickly shut it again. I wondered if she'd just remembered what I'd said about the days when she used to call Dad sweetie.

Looking a little surprised that there was no comeback, Dad shifted in his chair the way he was probably shifting his thinking. "That's a nice blouse, Lynn," he said. "Is it new?"

"Thanks," Mom said. "I'm glad you like it." I was proud of her for not telling him the blouse was at least two years old.

Maybe he hadn't noticed it before. Probably he hadn't even seen it. If Dad were home more often, like other husbands, he wouldn't have asked such a dumb question. I ached for Mom and the feelings of resentment toward Dad for being so obsessed with his work that he neglected his family.

The three of us managed to talk for a little while about nothing much, like, "Ms. Winn—you know, she teaches kindergarten—just had her baby . . . a girl."

And "How's everything going at school, Holly?"

I'd already dumped on Mom about school, and I had something more important I wanted to bring up with Dad. Ever since my conversation with Cody, his words sat like a rock in the pit of my stomach. He was counting on me to help him. I had to come through.

About the time I was beginning to wonder if

married people could just run out of things to talk about, Mom got up, rubbed the back of her neck, and announced, "School tomorrow. I need my sleep." She paused and added, "And so do you, Holly."

Dad moved to get up, but I quickly said, "In a minute, Mom. I need to talk to Dad."

"If this is about . . . ," Dad began, as Mom turned and walked upstairs.

"It won't take long. I promise," I begged. "First, I just want to know something about Cody inheriting his parents' money."

Dad settled back, but his tone was sharp. "Cody is too young to inherit. His attorney has petitioned the court, at Cody's request, to appoint Cody's uncle as his guardian."

"Cody said that his uncle was going to sell his house for him."

"I know nothing about that," Dad said, making it clear that he didn't care either. He looked at me sternly. "Your mother told me that Cody came to the house at your invitation, and she made it clear to you that my rule included *every* type of opportunity to see him. Have you broken the rule again?"

I couldn't help snapping back. "No! I was talking to Cody on the phone. I promised you I wouldn't go out with him, and I told Mom I wouldn't ask him again to come to the house. Dad, you can trust me."

"I know I can," he said. "I was out of line in asking." For a moment he squeezed his eyes shut and kneaded his forehead with his fingertips. When he relaxed and looked at me again, he said,

"Tell me, why are you asking about Cody's inheritance?"

"Sara told me that since Cody inherits a lot of money, it looks bad for him, but if Cody's too young to use the money he inherited, as you said, then getting the money can't possibly be a motive."

"I agree with you that getting the money wasn't a motive."

"You do?" I grinned. "Dad, does that mean you're beginning to think Cody's innocent?"

"I didn't say that," Dad told me, "but I don't think he killed his parents for their money. What I see is a spoiled kid in a fit of anger. He argued with his parents, and he lost control. When we get all the facts together, it's going to turn out to be as simple as that."

"You've got your mind made up already!" My heart was pounding, and I was so frightened I felt dizzy.

"Already? Most murder cases are either solved within the first few days or not at all." Dad hoisted himself out of his chair and stretched.

"Wait!" I cried. "I've got another question to ask you. Please!"

"All right. What is it?"

"Have the police checked the shops that sell doughnuts between here and the lake?"

"They've checked out every little food shop along the highway between Lake Conroe and Houston, and no one remembered Cody being there."

I gulped. "That doesn't mean anything one way or another. People forget. Maybe whoever waited on Cody was busy and just didn't remember him."

"Anything else?" Dad asked, and I could see exhaustion filming his eyes.

"Just one thing, and I think this is important." From my handbag I pulled the printouts from Mr. Garnett's computer. "Dad," I said, "Mr. Garnett made a lot of investments, according to Cody, and both Mrs. Garnett and Cody's uncle, Frank, objected to some of what he was doing. *Risky* and *shady*. Cody remembers them using those words. If he was involved in a shady business deal, then the people he was in partnership with, like the warehouse . . . I mean, if it was something illegal . . . well, what if one of them committed the murders and set things up so that Cody would look guilty?"

"A setup?"

"Yes!" I insisted. "If all the evidence makes Cody look guilty, only he isn't, then why couldn't it be a setup?"

"You're getting melodramatic, Holly." Dad's eyebrows dove downward into a scowl. "What are those papers? What have you got there?"

"Some personal records from Mr. Garnett's home computer about his business and income."

"Where did you get them?" Dad's voice was rising.

I tried to answer calmly. "Cody gave me permission to look through his father's computer."

As Dad's face grew red, I practically shouted. "Cody wasn't there! I went to the house with Sara!"

"You had no business in that house! And dragging your friend along is even more irresponsible, Holly."

"I had to go there! If you look at the warehouse figures, you'll see that they could be important! You can check them out—and the warehouse too." I waved the papers at Dad, and he took them, but he didn't bother to look at them.

"What did you think you were doing?"

"I was trying to find out who killed the Garnetts!" I yelled. "Which is what you should be doing! You weren't even interested in the other people in Mr. Garnett's life, you're so sure the murderer has to be Cody!"

"Holly!" Dad thundered. "This has gone far enough! I don't want to hear one more word about Cody! You're not an investigator! You're an emotional kid insisting on dangerously risking your life!"

"I'm not!" I shouted back. "I promised to help Cody prove that he's innocent."

"You're so obsessed with the idea of his innocence, you can't see straight."

I was so angry I saw Dad through a wavering red haze. "Obsessed?" I yelled at him. "Me? Look who's talking! *You're* the one who gets so obsessed with your cases that there's nothing else left in your life—especially Mom and me. You always put your job first! Always! Except for this time when

Cody needs you to find out who *really* killed his parents!"

Dad took a long breath, and when he spoke, his voice was so quiet I could hardly hear him. "Give it up, Holly," he said and thumped up the stairs.

I hunched up in my chair, slowing down from a full boil to a simmer. *Give it up? No way*, I told myself. Not when I knew I was right.

Chapter Eleven

T uesday. 8:30 A.M. School the next day was another bad dream. Sara just said, "Hi" and smiled—sort of—but she kept to herself. I shouldn't have been so rude to her, and I wanted to apologize, but I couldn't. She and Dad and the whole world could think Cody was guilty, but I'd promised to help him, even if it meant I had to do it all by myself.

I don't know what went on in any of my morning classes. I couldn't keep my mind on the subjects. Nothing made sense. All I could think about was Cody suffering through his parents' private funeral service, without friends to be with him, and all because of Mr. Ormond's decision. Mr. Ormond . . . It wasn't until the middle of French class that I knew I needed to talk to Cody's lawyer.

I realized that Monsieur Duprée had been calling my name when the kids sitting near me turned to stare. Somebody snickered.

"Faites attention, s'il vous plaît," my French teacher said.

"I don't know the answer," I told him.

"No answer is called for," he said. "The lunch bell's about to ring, and I asked you to remain a few minutes after class. I want to talk to you."

The bell clammered so loudly I jumped. As the rest of the class shot toward the door, I walked slowly up to Monsieur Duprée's desk.

He sat on the edge of the desk, facing me, and said, "Holly, I know that Cody is your friend, and with all the problems he's got right now, I can certainly understand why it's hard for you to keep your mind on your work."

I just nodded. There was nothing to say.

"I'm willing to let you make up the work, and I'm sure your other teachers will too, but right now the issue is you, yourself. Are you getting counseling?"

Surprised, I answered, "No. I don't need counseling. Cody's the one who needs help."

Monsieur Duprée's eyes were sympathetic. "Has he been arrested yet?"

"No! And he's not going to be! He's not guilty!"

I bowed my head, embarrassed. "I'm sorry I yelled," I said. "I'm trying hard to prove that Cody didn't commit the murders."

This time Monsieur Duprée was silent. When I finally looked up, I saw a deep concern in his eyes. "He didn't do it," I repeated.

"Do you really believe this? In spite of all the incriminating evidence we hear on the news?"

"I have to believe because I know it's true."

"Holly, your parents aren't allowing you to continue to see Cody, are they?" Monsieur Duprée asked, obviously concerned.

"No, they're not," I said, shivering as I remembered my father's angry face and words.

Monsieur Duprée stood, the relief that washed over his face gathering into a gentle smile. "I know this is a difficult time for you, but you're a girl with a strong purpose in life and good, common sense," he said. "I'm counting on you."

Like Cody is counting on me? For a moment the weight of what people expected and wanted of me was almost too much to bear. I reached out a hand and grasped the corner of Monsieur Duprée's desk, steadying myself.

"Now that you understand my concern, go on. Get your lunch," he said and smiled again.

"Thanks," I said. "I will."

But on the way downstairs I realized there were more important things to do than eat lunch. I hurried to the pay phones, looked up Paul Ormond's office number in the phone book, and placed a call.

His secretary told me that Mr. Ormond would be back from lunch in about forty-five minutes. I asked for a few minutes to see him and got an appointment, so I wrote down the address of his office. I didn't think twice about leaving school, as I ran toward the bus stop to go downtown.

As I reached the sidewalk, I heard Sara call, "Holly! Where are you going?"

I pretended I hadn't heard her. The only person I wanted to talk to right now was Paul Ormond.

Mr. Ormond's office was small and plain, which surprised me, but it was on the twenty-fifth floor and had a window wall with a great view of Buffalo Bayou and the theater district. The cars on the streets looked like minitoys, and the pedestrians seemed so tiny and insignificant I wondered if they were real people with real problems.

Mr. Ormond strode in and shook my hand heartily. "Cody has told me all about you," he said.

Mr. Ormond was young and had the same shade of tan that Frank Baker had, but he'd lost a lot of his dark hair. His tie had bright flags and pennants on it and clashed with his suit. I felt a rush of disappointment. I guess I had hoped to see someone with the poise and forcefulness of an attorney in a TV show.

"Sit down, Holly," Mr. Ormond said as he waved a hand at his only visitor's chair. He slid into the chair behind his desk, leaned his elbows on the desk, and smiled at me. "Tell me you can give Cody an alibi," he said.

"I wish I could, but I can't," I answered.

He shrugged and continued to smile, which

bothered me. Cody was his client and was suspected of murder. The least Mr. Ormond could do would be to look serious, if not sympathetic.

I felt uncomfortable, as if we'd started all wrong, so I tried again. "I would have liked to come to the funeral service," I said.

Shrugging again, Mr. Ormond said, "According to Frank, Cody didn't want anyone to be there."

"But I thought that the private service was *your* decision."

"Nope. Cody's," he answered. "And he was probably right. He broke down and cried all the way through it."

Why didn't Cody tell me how he felt? I wondered. *Why say it was his attorney's idea?* I burned with guilt for doubting him, as I realized that Cody may have wanted to be alone with his sorrow but was embarrassed to say so.

"So tell me why you came to see me," Mr. Ormond said.

"I'm trying to find a way to help Cody," I told him. "I thought if I could find out what you're doing for Cody . . . I mean, if I told you what I know, and we thought about this together, we could come up with something that might help."

Mr. Ormond looked at his watch. "I've got an appointment in fifteen minutes," he said. "Can we keep it brief?"

Whatever I wanted to talk over with him went out of my mind. Instead I demanded, "Are you an experienced criminal defense attorney?"

He answered slowly. "I've had a few cases— mostly assignments from the court, in which I've represented some defendants who were up on burglary charges. They were too poor to hire an attorney."

"What happened to them?"

I thought he smirked as he said, "What else? They were guilty, which wasn't any surprise to the juries, and they were sent off to serve time."

I kept cool and instead of asking, "What good did you do them?" I continued, "Did you handle any murder cases?"

"Nope." He cocked his head and studied me, a slow grin buttering his lips. "Does it matter?"

I sat up a little straighter. "It's going to matter a lot to Cody! What are you doing to help prove he's innocent so he won't be arrested?"

"It's not my job to keep him from being arrested or to prove he's innocent. It's my job to defend his rights when he comes to trial."

When he comes to trial! My ears began to buzz, and for a moment I grew so dizzy it was hard to focus my eyes. Mr. Ormond believed Cody was guilty!

"You okay?" Mr. Ormond asked. "You look a little pale. Want a drink of water?"

I shook my head and took a deep breath, pulling myself together. "*If* Cody is arrested, how are you going to prove he's not guilty?"

"I don't have to prove he's not guilty. I don't even have to present a case. It's up to the prosecutor to make a strong enough case to convince a jury that Cody's guilty. So far, the police have nothing against him but circumstantial evidence." He smiled. "Lucky for Cody there was no one around who could place him at the scene of the crime, and the police haven't been able to turn up the murder weapon."

I caught my breath, suddenly hopeful. "Are you saying there's a good chance he can't be convicted if all the evidence is just circumstantial?"

"Unfortunately, that's not the way it works," he said. "There's a lot against Cody—his returning to the house, arguing with his parents and threatening them, his unproven whereabouts at the lake. . . . He stacked the deck against himself pretty thoroughly."

He looked at his watch again and got up, which meant I had to leave. "Don't worry so much, Holly," Mr. Ormond said. "Frank Baker's a good friend, and I'll do my best to help his nephew. Trust me."

I wasn't about to trust Mr. Ormond in anything he said or did. The express elevator that took me to the lobby plunged downward as fast as my spirits. As I searched my mind frantically, wondering what I could possibly do next, the answer came to me. Much as I dreaded what might take place, I knew there was only one option left. I walked down to the corner and caught a bus for West University. I was on my way to visit Glenda Jordan.

*T*uesday. 3:15 P.M. As I walked from the bus stop to Glenda's street, I thought of a dozen reasons why I should change my mind, turn around, and go home. For one thing, I hadn't telephoned.

Maybe Glenda was out. Grocery shopping? Yes. This was a good time to grocery-shop. And I shouldn't have come alone. Maybe Sara . . . No. This was something I had to do alone.

My back was damp with sweat as I reached the shaded oasis of Glenda Jordan's front yard. As I followed the curling, winding path to the door, my nervousness slid away. By the time I rang the bell, my mind and body were as numb as a tooth that's been prepped for a filling.

Glenda opened the door and smiled. "Come in," she said. No questions, no surprise at seeing me. It gave me a strange feeling of comfort.

I sat next to her on the sofa, soaking in the blue-green-gold light until I was at peace.

"You invited me to go to the Garnetts' house with you," I said.

"Yes," she answered. She looked at my hair and smiled a satisfied smile. "You're wearing the amber barrette. Good."

I knew the amber, pressed against my hair, would be growing warm. My scalp tingled, but I resisted the impulse to reach up and touch the stone. I asked Glenda, "When . . . when should we go?"

"Do you still have a key?"

I nodded, and she said, "Then we should visit the house as soon as possible. Are you ready?"

"Yes." My whisper was so soft I repeated myself, but Glenda was already on her feet.

"We will enter the house through the back door," she said, "because that is the door through which the murderer entered and left."

I winced. The back door in most houses was the one used by members of the family.

Glenda paused on the doorstep and turned her dark eyes full upon me. "The answer we receive may not be to your liking," she said.

I bristled. "Cody didn't kill his parents!"

"Be calm," she cautioned. "In your search for the truth, you must keep an open mind. Otherwise our attempt to learn the answers will be of no use at all."

"I'm sorry," I mumbled. "I do want to learn the truth. That's why I'm here." I pulled the key from the pocket of my jeans and opened the back door.

As we stepped inside, I shivered with a chill that didn't come from the air conditioners, and I almost lost my nerve. But Glenda put a firm hand on my arm. "There is nothing to be afraid of. You are sensitive to what happened in this house because you arrived open-minded and receptive to whatever you may encounter."

"When I was here before, I wasn't afraid."

"That's because you entered the house with a different purpose. This time you have come to make contact with those who violently left this plane of existence. You came to seek these spirits, and you have reached them. They know."

Legs wobbling, I allowed myself to be led through the kitchen and den and on into the living room, dim with its drapes cutting off much of the light. I stopped at the door, horrified when I saw ugly, dried brown splatters on some of the furniture and one of the walls. Fortunately, someone had laid towels over a section of the carpet, covering the spot where the murders must have taken place. The sofas crouched like large, sleeping cats, and the baby-grand piano was a dark mound in the corner. I wavered, closing my eyes, repelled by the sight and by the room's cloying, musty-sweet smell.

"It's good that we were able to come before the room was cleaned," Glenda said. She propelled me toward a pair of wing chairs on the far side of the room and plopped me down into the nearer one. She took the other. Between us was only a small table on which rested a vase of artificial flowers and a telephone. She pulled a small tape recorder from her pocket, placed it on the table, and turned it on. "I hope you don't mind," she said. "It's important to record these sessions so they may be studied later."

I shrugged. "Okay," I said.

"Relax," Glenda told me. "Stop clutching the arms of the chair. Place your hands in your lap, palms up." As I obeyed, she said, "Fine. Now begin with your toes and work up to your head. Think about each part of your body and help it to relax."

She began to chant a little singsong relaxation formula, and I found myself falling into the spell. I sunk against the back of the chair, my shoulders sagged, and my breathing became light and shallow.

Soon after Glenda had finished her chant, the downstairs air conditioner cycled off, and the house was totally silent. I listened for the sound of a car on the street, or the caw of a grackle, or a dog's bark; but the Garnetts' house and all that surrounded it were silent. I shivered, wondering what would happen next.

Glenda's whisper broke the silence so unexpectedly that I cried out.

"Mr. and Mrs. Garnett, we are here only to help. We want to make known the identity of the one who murdered you," she said. She stared into the room, and I squinted at the point on which her gaze was fixed. I didn't see anything.

"Are you here with us?" Glenda asked.

So—she hadn't seen them either. I began breathing again.

"Speak to them," Glenda said to me in that awful whisper that seemed louder than a shout. "Tell them who you are and why you are here."

"M-Mr. and Mrs. Garnett," I began, but I choked up. I coughed and had to start again. "Please, Mr. and Mrs. Garnett," I whispered, gripping the chair arms so tightly my fingers ached. "I'm Holly Campbell. You know me. I'm a friend of Cody's. I'm trying to prove that he's innocent of your m-murder. He is, isn't he? Please, isn't he? Can you tell me?"

The silence in the house was so thick I could hear my own heartbeat. No one spoke. Nothing happened.

"Holly, close your eyes and picture the way this room was the last time you saw it," Glenda said. "Picture the people in it. Try to remember the conversation. Relive it."

I did, vividly recalling my last visit here. I'd been invited for dinner. Mr. Garnett, who'd pulled into his shell like a grumpy turtle, hadn't added much to the conversation. As soon as we had finished dessert, he left the dining room and entered his office, shutting the door firmly behind him. Mrs. Garnett had shooed Cody and me out of the kitchen, insisting that it only took one person to put dishes into a dishwasher.

"Let's find some music to dance to," Cody had said and led me toward the living room. As he opened a cabinet and pulled out some CDs, I perched on the piano bench and poked at the two top keys.

"Can you play the piano?" I'd asked.

"I took lessons when I was a kid," he'd answered, "only because my mom made me, but I hated piano lessons, so I've forgotten everything except 'Chopsticks.'"

"I took ballet," I had said and chuckled. "Every little girl on my block took ballet. We were all skinny arms and legs, and our mothers were probably desperate for us to become graceful."

"Why do parents do it?" he'd asked.

"Do what?"

"Try to run their kids' lives?"

I had been surprised at the bitterness in his voice. "It's not running their lives," I'd said. "It's giving kids advantages and trying to prepare them for when they grow up."

"Growing up won't come soon enough for me," Cody had said. He put a CD in the entertainment center and held out his arms. "Right music, right girl. C'mon, Holly. Let's dance."

I could hear the music swirling throughout the

room. It was the same soft sound Cody had chosen that night, but now it seemed harsher and louder.

Uncomfortable at the memory, I shifted in my chair. The vision of Cody faded, but the music went on relentlessly, pulling me into the present.

My eyes shot open as the music pounded inside my head. The room was filled with a suffocating, possessive greed, so intense that the air grew red, and the horrible smell of death was sickening. A whirlpool of horror and evil swirled around me, hot against the back of my neck and prickling up and down my arms. I sensed that someone was coming . . . coming from the hallway . . . coming closer . . . and closer . . .

I knew that at any moment someone I had good reason to fear was going to step through the doorway and meet me face-to-face.

Chapter Twelve

The telephone next to my chair rang shrilly, shattering the vision. I leaped to my feet and screamed, holding my ears as the telephone's jangle beat against them.

Heedlessly I ran through the front doorway, tripped over the brick edging on the walk, and fell facedown on the lawn. I didn't even try to get up. I just lay there and sobbed. I had come so close— so very close—to receiving the answer to my question, but I hadn't had the courage to stay in that room another minute.

As my sobs became dry shudders, Glenda spoke, and I raised my head to see that she was sitting cross-legged next to me, her hands clasped calmly in her lap. "Lock the door," she said. "We must leave the house exactly as we found it."

I scrambled to my feet and did as she said. The street was quiet. Either away at their jobs or safely wrapped in the insulating hum of their air conditioners, no one had heard the commotion I'd made, and I was grateful.

I slowly walked back to Glenda and sat beside her. Nervously plucking at the long blades of grass, I asked the question over and over in my mind. Finally I was able to say it aloud. "What did you see?"

"Nothing," she said. "You were the one who asked to be shown the answer. I was there simply to guide you."

I looked up quickly, but her features were soft and blank. "Didn't you feel something . . . anything?" I asked. The fear returned, and I shuddered.

"It was your experience, not mine," Glenda said. "Tell me—what did you learn?"

I drew up my knees and rested my arms and head on them. "Nothing!" I groaned. "I really blew it. The music was loud and horrible. Then the room got red and hot with a sickening, evil greed, and I knew that someone was coming. I could feel him coming from the den toward the room, and soon I'd see his face. Then the phone rang, and it was like someone screaming at me to run! Run away! I was never so scared in my life. I couldn't take it."

I looked up into Glenda's dark, impassive eyes and groaned again. "I might have found out what I wanted to know, but I ruined everything."

"Not necessarily," she said. "Maybe deep inside your mind you know who was going to come into the room."

154

"No! I don't!"

"You said you could 'feel him coming.' How do you know the person you sensed was male?"

Stunned by her question, I tried to think. Slowly the answer came to me. "Footsteps. I heard footsteps. They were measured and heavy—at least heavier than a woman's would be."

"You used the word *greed*.

"Yes."

"Greed is a loathsome thing. It chews at a conscience until it has devoured it, because it is desperate for possessions it does not have."

Cody? No! I quickly told myself that it wasn't greedy of Cody to want a new car. His Thunderbird was so old it constantly needed repairs. Wanting a new car was just a normal feeling. It wasn't greed. It wasn't!

Glenda's question broke into my thoughts. "What else did you learn?"

"Nothing."

I waited for her to say something else, but she didn't, so I got up and brushed some grass from my jeans. "I've got to get home," I said. "I might have to wait awhile for the bus."

As Glenda rose gracefully, I searched for the right words. I'd choke on saying, "Thank you." It would be weird to thank her for giving me the most awful experience of my life. "It was . . . uh . . . good of you to come with me," I finally said.

"You have proved to both of us that you are receptive," Glenda told me. "If you wish, we'll try the experiment again."

"I—I can't."

155

"You feel this way now, but when the memory is not as vivid, you'll change your mind."

"I won't! Believe me, I won't."

I broke into a trot and made it over to the boulevard in time to catch my bus.

Exhausted, I leaned against the window. I knew I should think about what had happened. Maybe something else would come to me, but I pushed away the thoughts. I couldn't take them. Not now.

When I finally arrived home, I carefully locked the door behind me and pulled the amber barrette from my hair. I wanted to destroy it, to stomp on it, to throw it far, far away. But Mom had given it to me. It had been a special gift, given in love.

Frustrated, I ran to the living room and shoved the barrette deep down inside the back of the sofa. Nobody would ever find it there. I'd never wear it again.

I jumped at the sound of the front-door bell, but I could see Sara trying to peer into the window next to the door, so I hurried to the door and opened it.

"You look terrible," Sara said. Then she stepped inside and hugged me.

I hugged her back. "I'm sorry I was such a dork," I told her.

"You weren't a dork. I was coming down too hard on you."

"It's my fault. I shouldn't have lost my temper."

She stepped back and smiled. The smile was just what I needed.

"Your hair's a mess. It's all over your face," she said. "Where's that barrette you usually wear?"

I looked away. "Gone," I said.

"Well, get your hairbrush and another barrette, and I'll fix your hair for you."

We ran upstairs. I pulled a large white plastic barrette from my drawer and sat on the bed while Sara brushed my hair.

"Where have you been?" she asked. "I saw you leaving early, and when I got home after school, I phoned everywhere I could think of trying to find you."

I shrugged. "I went to see Cody's lawyer."

"Oh?"

"I don't like him, Sara. I don't think he's going to help Cody at all."

"You were there a long time. Did he talk about what he can do for Cody?"

"So far he doesn't have any plans." Sara closed the barrette with a snap, so I twisted around to face her. "He only let me stay a few minutes."

"Then where have you been? I've been worried about you."

Sara's my best friend, I told myself. *She'll understand. But I can't talk about what happened. I only want to forget it.*

Then, all of a sudden, I broke down and the whole story poured out, from the moment I entered the Garnetts' house with Glenda.

As she listened, wide-eyed, Sara grew pale.

"Someone was coming to the doorway," I said, "and I waited. I couldn't move. But then the phone rang."

"Oh!" Sara said. She looked sick.

"I screamed, and it all fell apart—the music, the horror—it disappeared. All I wanted to do was get out of that house, so I ran." I sighed. "One minute more—just one minute, and I might have seen the murderer's face. Oh, Sara, I came so close and ruined everything because I was such a coward!"

"You weren't a coward." Sara got to her feet and stared out of the window, her back to me. "Will you get mad at me if I tell you that I don't think anything happened in that house, that Glenda Jordan just used the power of suggestion, and you fell into it?"

"Sara, I know what I saw and heard."

"You saw and heard the things you wanted to see and hear." She turned to face me. "Holly, you've got a good imagination, and Glenda used it. She's weird. She's probably harmless, and that's the only reason she hasn't been locked up. This awful thing she did with you had to have been some kind of great ego game for her. You're probably the only person in the world who believes her. I bet her ego's puffed up like a balloon."

"No, Sara."

"Yes, it's true. Tell me, what did you really see?"

"The room with the bloodstains."

"Didn't you see the same thing when you came into the room, before you had your so-called vision?"

"I guess. But the vision was different."

158

"How?"

"This time the air was red, like when you're under a red sunlamp, and I felt . . . well, I felt all around me a kind of horror and greed."

"Greed?" Sara's eyes narrowed and she stared at me unbelievingly. "How can you feel greed?"

"I can't explain it."

Sara came to sit beside me and took my hands. "Of course you can't explain it. Your mind was full of strange ideas that crazy woman put into it."

"She didn't."

"She did." Sara's eyes filled with concern. "You're so desperate to prove that Cody's innocent, you're not stopping to think. You're ready to jump at anything that might help him—no matter how weird. You have to admit that this séance kind of thing you got into was *really* weird."

"You weren't there," I said. "You don't understand. It was all happening the way it was supposed to. If I'd just stayed . . . If only the phone hadn't rung when it did . . ."

That strange, sick look flashed over Sara's face again, and I gasped as I realized why. "*You're* the one who phoned, weren't you?" I demanded. "You said you were calling everyplace, trying to find me! It was you!"

"I did call the Garnetts' house," Sara said. "I was worried about you, Holly. I was terribly afraid you'd really do what you said you'd do and go into that house with Glenda. And you shouldn't."

"How could you do this to me?"

"I told you—because I was worried about you."

"But you ruined it!" Tears began rolling down my cheeks, and I wiped them away with the back of my hands.

"I'm sorry, Holly," Sara said, and she looked as miserable as I felt. "But believe me, please! I honestly don't think there was anything there to ruin —just Glenda's power of suggestion that had you going. You went there because you were desperate to help Cody. I called because I was desperate to find you."

Under a stack of notebook paper on my desk, I found a box of tissues. I mopped my face and blew my nose before I turned to Sara. "We didn't get very far, did we? Either of us?"

"I don't know," Sara said quietly. "Maybe my phone call stopped you from seeing something you shouldn't have seen."

"I thought you didn't believe that—"

"Let me finish," she said. "I was going to say that it stopped you from seeing whatever Glenda Jordan wanted you to see." Sara paused. "Are you mad at me now?"

"No," I said as I sank down on the bed. "I'm too tired inside to be mad at anybody."

Sara reached over and touched my barrette. "I'm glad your amber barrette's gone. See, it proves that Glenda was wrong when she said that stupid stuff about your being an amber girl."

I slid off the bed. "Let's go downstairs and get some Cokes."

As we settled into the glider on the screened porch, Sara said, "Sherry's mother is giving her a birthday party. It's supposed to be a date party, but right now there's nobody I like enough to ask. Why don't we go together and just hang out?"

"I wasn't invited," I said.

"You know you will be. You probably left school before Sherry had a chance to ask you.

"The problem is that the kids don't know how to act around you or what to do with you, Holly. Maybe if you could talk to people or joke a little bit, like you normally do, they'll relax. You're just so . . . well, obsessed with Cody that you've shut everybody out."

"Obsessed? That's a strong word to use," I said. "I'm just trying to prove that Cody's innocent."

"Why can't you leave that up to the police—to your dad?"

"Because he isn't keeping an open mind. He thinks this kind of killing fits a pattern."

Sara was silent for a moment. Finally she asked, "How much do you care about Cody?"

"I don't know," I said.

She sat up, hope in her eyes. "Then you aren't in love with him?"

"We've been friends for four years, and before all this happened, I liked him a lot. That's all."

"Before?"

"I mean, I like him. But that's not why I'm trying to help him. It's a matter of fairness. A person is supposed to be thought of as innocent unless proven guilty, but everyone has taken it for granted that Cody is guilty, right from the beginning."

"Face facts, Holly. You don't know for sure if he's guilty or innocent."

"He said he didn't do it."

Sara nodded. "I understand how you feel," she said. "But please, Holly, please don't take chances! Let your dad handle the investigation without your help."

Dad showed up at the house before Mom, who had some errands to run after school. It was my night to make dinner, and, when he walked into the kitchen, I was busy stirring a Stroganoff sauce to pour over the meatballs that were browning in the cast-iron frying pan.

Dad sniffed the air and smiled. "Smells wonderful. When do we eat?"

"In about half an hour, when Mom gets home."

"You're a good cook, Holly. Almost as good a cook as your mother."

"Tell her that sometime," I said.

As Dad slipped off his gun and shoulder holster and laid them on the counter, he looked surprised. "What?"

"When's the last time you told Mom she's a good cook?"

He didn't answer, so I said, "So, tell her. She'd like to hear it."

Dad gulped down a long drink of water. "It's hot out there," he said. "Another month, at least, before it'll begin to turn cool."

I just nodded and kept stirring the sauce. Dad wasn't still mad at me, and I was glad about that. In fact, he seemed to be in a particularly good mood.

162

"Holly," he said, "as I told you before, there was absolutely no excuse for you entering the Garnetts' house and accessing his computer."

"Dad—"

He held up a hand for silence. "However," he said, "I looked into the information on the printouts you gave me, and it seems that the FBI has been interested in Sam Garnett's partner and his activities. To make a long story short, the warehouse is being used to store counterfeit materials —stuff like fake name-brand watches and handbags."

I dropped the spoon and gasped. "Mr. Garnett was a criminal?"

"Let's put it this way: He was allegedly involved in illegal activities."

"Dad! You see what this means? He was hanging out with criminals. One of them killed him! Not Cody!" I began to walk back and forth as ideas popped into my head. "Mr. Garnett opened the door—that's why there was no sign that someone had entered illegally. He knew the guy who had rung the bell, so he opened the door and let him in. But this guy hadn't come to socialize, or to talk business. Mr. Garnett was cheating him, and he was angry. He'd come to kill him. Then Mrs. Garnett walked in and saw what had happened, and she was killed too!"

"Holly," Dad said. "Sit down. Take it easy. It didn't happen that way."

"How do you know?"

"There's a network behind the smuggling, with operations in other states as well, but there's nothing to indicate that Garnett wasn't cooperating with the organization."

"What about Mr. Garnett's partner?"

"Unavailable at the moment," Dad said. "He may have seen what was coming and left town in a hurry. They'll find him."

"He may not have left town," I said. "And even if Mr. Garnett was cooperating with the organization of crooks, he still could have had trouble with his partner, couldn't he?"

"It's possible."

"And his partner could be the murderer, just as I said."

Dad sighed. "It's possible, but not logical. You're fishing, Holly. Sooner or later you're going to have to face facts. You're at a dead end. Everything we've turned up points to Cody."

At the dinner table Mom raved about the Stroganoff.

"Like yours," Dad managed to say as he stared into his plate. "You're a good cook, too, Lynn."

"Why, thank you," Mom said. I could hear both surprise and pleasure in her voice.

I don't know what the Stroganoff tasted like. I gulped down a couple of bites, but I could hardly eat.

Mom took her dishes to the sink, then sat down facing me. "Holly," she said, "Monsieur Duprée telephoned me today. He's worried about you. He thinks you should get counseling."

"I don't need counseling," I answered. "All I'm

164

trying to do is help Cody, and everyone is making such a big deal out of it!"

"I understand you didn't show up for any of your afternoon classes."

Dad put down his fork. As they both waited for what I'd say, I felt like their eyes were drilling little holes in my forehead.

"Okay. I'll tell you where I was. I went to see Cody's lawyer. His name is Paul Ormond. I hoped we could talk about helping Cody, but he wasn't interested. He isn't doing a thing to try to prove that Cody is innocent. I bet he isn't even a very good trial lawyer."

Mom sighed. "Holly, you can't think straight about the situation because you've become so obsessed with trying to uncover some unknown suspect."

"I'm obsessed?" I choked on a laugh. Couldn't anyone understand what I was trying to do?

Dad looked at Mom. "Sometimes you've used that term for me when I'm working hard on a case."

At first, Mom looked flustered, but she quickly straightened up and said, "Yes, when you're unable to think about anything else . . . when you're behaving like Holly is now."

"I can't help it," I told them. "I feel like I'm racing with a time bomb that won't stop ticking. It scares me, because I know I've got to help Cody before the time runs out."

"Holly," Dad said softly. He took my hand and held it tightly. "Holly, I'm sorry, but time has already run out."

Chapter Thirteen

Wednesday. 8:30 A.M. When I first got to school, Sara had been standing in front of my locker, waiting for me. During the day I tried to pay attention to what was going on in my classes. I know Monsieur Duprée meant well, but I didn't want anyone else worrying about me and calling Mom. I even hung around with some of my friends and talked a lot of trivia. With Sara there to help me, it wasn't too hard.

Sara had the Jeep, so after school she drove me home. She started talking about this awful movie her family had rented and making up goofy dialogue for some of the scenes, so by the time we entered our house, I was laughing. But I had no sooner put down my books than the phone rang.

"Hi," I said.

The only answer was silence.

I was about to hang up, thinking it was either one of those computerized sales pitches that hadn't kicked in or the beginning of an obscene call, when Cody said, "Holly, it's me."

"Cody?" I repeated, and from the corner of my eyes I saw Sara stiffen to attention. "Where are you?" I asked.

"At Uncle Frank's," he said. "At least for now. That's what I wanted to talk to you about. Frank went downtown to talk to Mr. Ormond. Some woman called the police and said she saw me around ten o'clock Friday night in a convenience store over on Kirby. But she's wrong! I wasn't there!"

Cody's voice broke and he began to cry.

"Don't cry. It's going to be all right," I kept saying, while at the same time I thought, *Where did this woman suddenly come from? And what makes her think she saw Cody? Lots of teenage guys are his height and coloring.*

Finally Cody stopped crying and said, "Holly, they're going to arrest me. I know they will."

"Not yet," I insisted. "All the evidence so far is circumstantial. The police don't have a murder weapon, and they don't have an eyewitness who can place you at the scene."

"I don't know how much this woman told them. She could have made up anything."

"The police get a lot of false identifications, even a lot of false confessions. They know how to sort through them."

Cody was under control now, but I could hear the despair in his voice. "I can't take the chance," he said.

My fingers gripped the phone so hard they hurt. "What do you mean?"

"I don't want to be arrested. I couldn't take being in jail—especially for something I didn't do."

"Cody! What are you talking about?"

"You and Uncle Frank are the only ones who believed in me."

"We still believe in you."

"I know I can trust you not to tell anyone that I called. You said you'd help me. Well, that's the best way you can help right now."

"Cody, why . . . ?"

"I've got to go now, Holly," he said. "I thought . . . well . . . that I owed it to you to say good-bye."

"Cody, no!" I shrieked. "Wait! Don't do anything you shouldn't. Let me come and talk to you."

"It won't do any good."

"Please," I begged. "Please just do this as a favor to me."

For a moment he was silent. Then he said, "You'll have to come soon."

"I will. I promise. Wait. Just wait. I'll be at your uncle's house within twenty . . . *fifteen* minutes."

As we hung up, I turned to Sara. "Cody's in terrible shape. He doesn't know what he's doing," I told her. "He said he owed it to me to say goodbye. He may be running away or . . . or . . ."

"Suicide?" Sara gasped and said, "Call somebody! 911? Your dad?"

I grabbed her shoulders. "I can't. Cody said he trusted me not to tell anyone. And he promised he wouldn't do anything until I got to his uncle's house and had a chance to talk to him. Take me there, Sara. Please?"

She hesitated. "You said he doesn't know what he's doing. What if he's dangerous?"

"I'll go in alone. You stay outside."

"I can't let you do that. I'll—"

"Sara!" I shouted. "We haven't got time to argue about it. Take me to Cody. Please!"

"C'mon," Sara said. She picked up her purse and car keys and hurried toward the back door. I was right behind her.

Sara made it to Frank Baker's house in a little under fifteen minutes. We didn't talk. Sara concentrated on her driving, while I just hung on and hoped and prayed that Cody hadn't done anything desperate.

As we pulled up in front of the house, Sara gave a sigh or relief. She pointed to Cody's car in the driveway and said, "Look! The trunk's open. That means he's running away."

I leaped out of the car and ran up the driveway to the back door. It was ajar, so I pushed it open and dashed into the kitchen—its walls so cluttered with sieves and stirring spoons and

169

knives and pans, it was distracting. I wished I could tear them all down and throw them away. A suitcase was open on the kitchen table, and a rolled sleeping bag was on the floor beside it. "Cody!" I yelled. "It's me—Holly. Where are you?"

Cody bounded into the room and stopped. He was pale, and his eyes were red and swollen. "Holly," he said, "you shouldn't have come. I told you—it won't do any good."

"You can't run!" I said. "If you do, then everyone will be positive that you're guilty."

"They are already." He stood in front of me, took my hands, and looked into my eyes. "Holly, I appreciate your standing by me more than you'll ever know, so I want to be honest with you. There's something I have to tell you."

At that moment Sara walked through the kitchen door, and Cody stiffened. "What are *you* doing here?" he asked her.

Sara's chin lifted defensively. "I drove Holly here—even though I tried to talk her out of coming."

Cody took a step back, away from me. "You said you wouldn't tell anyone."

"Sara was there when you telephoned. She couldn't help but hear some of what we were talking about. I didn't have time to call a cab, so I asked Sara to drive me."

Cody frowned at Sara. She glared back, giving a kick to the sleeping bag. "It's cowardly to run away," she said.

"So I'm a coward," Cody growled, "and

quit kicking that sleeping bag. It belongs to my uncle."

"Cody, please listen to me," I said. "You can't run away."

"You were going to help me," he said accusingly, "and what have you come up with? Nothing!"

"I tried. I'm still trying."

"Trying's not enough. If I stick around, they're gong to arrest me."

"Cody, they don't even have the murder weapon. But if you—"

"Shut up! Just shut up!" Cody strode to the table, elbowed Sara out of the way, and slammed the lid on his suitcase.

I saw a pair of jeans lying on one of the chairs, so I picked them up and threw them at him. "If you're going to do something so idiotic and stupid, at least do it right."

Cody held the jeans a moment, and I could see him trying to calm down. I knew he was too frightened to think clearly, and I was ashamed at losing my temper.

Pointing to a rip in one leg, Cody said, "I meant to try to mend that, but now I don't have time. Dumb dog."

"Tiger?" I asked.

"Yeah, Tiger."

Sara's eyes narrowed. "Tiger," she said. "Isn't he the dog that belongs to the neighbors who lived behind Mr. Arlington's house?"

"That's right," I told her. "If Tiger bites, they shouldn't let him run loose."

"They never let him run loose," Cody said. He folded the jeans, added them to the other things in his suitcase, and snapped it shut again. "Dumb dog—they treat him like a baby. He's never allowed outside their backyard."

Sara spoke slowly. "In the early newspaper stories, your neighbor, Mr. Arlington, said he saw someone jump the back fence, and the people who own Tiger said he barked at someone in their backyard. Cody, when were you in your neighbors' backyard with Tiger?"

I felt the way I had one summer picnic when the kid next door dumped a whole glass of ice cubes down my back. I was frozen. I couldn't move. And the pain from the cold was unbearable. "Cody?" I whispered. There was nothing else to say.

Cody held on to the back of a chair, his head bent as he seemed to study his shoes. At last he straightened, turned, and looked at me. "Don't think it, Holly," he said and laughed bitterly. "It didn't happen the night my parents were murdered. It happened a few days before that. Mrs. Rollins didn't want to pay a plumber to fix a dripping pipe in the backyard, so she asked me to do it. Tiger got out and went after me before she could catch him."

"I'm sorry," I said. "I shouldn't have asked. It doesn't matter."

"It does matter. It's one more piece of the so-called evidence that's piling up against me. Nobody will believe me. They'll just believe what they want—that I'm guilty. Can't you see, that's why I have to get out of here? I don't have a chance."

The phone rang, and we all jumped. Cody grabbed for it, and the caller must have had a lot to say, because it took awhile for Cody to answer. "I've got to get away from here, Uncle Frank. . . . I know we talked about it, but . . ." Cody threw a quick glance in Sara's direction. "I can't tell you. . . . It's no use. I've made up my mind. . . . It won't do any good to . . . I haven't got time now." Finally he said, "Thanks, Uncle Frank. Thanks for everything. Goodbye."

As he hung up, I begged, "Listen to your uncle, Cody. Listen to me."

"I haven't got time to argue with you, Holly," Cody said. "The police are on their way with a warrant to search this house. An anonymous caller gave them some kind of information that Frank said was 'probable cause.' Uncle Frank called from Mr. Ormond's car. They're trying to get here before the police do."

"It doesn't matter if they search! You haven't anything to hide!"

"Do you think that makes any difference?" Cody swept up his suitcase and the sleeping bag. "Uncle Frank said I'll probably be arrested. I'm not going to jail, Holly! I can't go to jail!"

He turned and ran out the back door.

I started after him, but Sara grabbed my arm. "We can't let him go!" I shouted at her.

"Don't make him any more angry than he is," Sara said. "He's not thinking straight. He could go out of control."

As I tried to get to the door, she hung on. I could see fear in her eyes. "Sara, he won't hurt us!" I cried.

We heard the tires on Cody's car squeal as it shot out of the driveway. Sara let go of my arm. Exhausted, I dropped into the nearest kitchen chair.

Sara glanced around nervously. "We should get out of here. We don't belong in this house, and with the police coming . . ."

We heard the cars arrive. "It's too late," I said and got to my feet. "All we can do is explain why we're here." It sounded easy, but I dreaded having to face my father.

Dad and Bill arrived with half a dozen backup police. At first, Dad stared at me as if he couldn't believe what he was seeing, but his eyes turned hard, and he snapped, "Where's Cody?"

"He left," I said.

"Do you know where he was going?"

"No."

Dad looked so angry that Sara clutched my hand. Her voice shaking, she said, "Honest, Mr. Campbell. Cody was awfully upset. He just ran out the door. He didn't tell us anything except that he didn't want to be arrested."

"Put out an APB," Dad snapped at one of the uniformed officers. "Tell them to double-check the Garnetts' house in West U and in Lake Conroe."

The man left to use a police radio. I could hear the crackle and the voices out on the driveway.

Frank and Mr. Ormond burst through the door

174

and into the overcrowded kitchen. Bill pulled out a warrant, handing it to Frank, and three officers left the kitchen, fanning out through the rest of the house.

I pressed against the wall, hoping to slip out of the house while there was so much confusion, but no such luck. The moment the kitchen began to empty, Dad turned to me with such a stern look that all I wanted to do was get out of there—fast!

"Sara needs to get home," I said and tried to edge past Dad.

"Sara may be excused, but you stay right where you are," Dad said. "What I have to say won't take long."

"I'll wait for you in the car," Sara said and was out the back door before I could answer.

I walked to the sink, reached into a cupboard, and pulled out a glass. The jumble of hardware hanging on the wall gave me a headache, and I needed a drink of water.

"You gave me your word you wouldn't see Cody," Dad said.

I drank some of the water and turned to face him. "Until this afternoon I've kept my word to you and to Mom. But when Cody called and said goodbye, it frightened me—Sara too. Just ask her. We didn't know what he was going to do. He told me he'd wait for me only a little while. I didn't have time to try to find you and ask your permission. Mom either."

"You could have called 911."

"I couldn't. Cody just said goodbye. He didn't

tell me what he had in mind. What if he was thinking about committing suicide and he heard sirens and knew the police were coming to his house? He might have panicked."

Dad didn't answer. He stared at a spot on the wall near the top of my head.

I tried again. "I thought I was doing what was right, Dad. I didn't know what else to do."

"It's the same set," Dad said.

"What?"

He walked toward me, took a handkerchief from his pocket, and reached over my head. With the handkerchief covering his fingers, Dad pulled a ten-inch butcher knife from a rack on the wall.

I twisted around to watch, gasping as I saw the black-and-white bone handles and the empty slot third from the left. "It's exactly like that knife set in the Garnetts' house!" I exclaimed.

Dad studied the knife, turning it over and over in his hands. The blade was shining, but in the crevice next to the handle, I could see a few tiny streak of rust. Rust? No. I pressed a hand against my stomach and fought back a wave of nausea. Those streaks weren't rust. They were blood.

"Looks like we have the murder weapon," Dad said.

"It can't be," I murmured. "Cody wouldn't have put the weapon in such an obvious place."

"It probably didn't seem obvious to him. He probably thought he was being clever, switching knives and burying the clean one to distract us. A lot of criminals do some pretty dumb things, like

176

leaving bloody clothing where it can easily be found, or burying it with the murder weapon in a backyard, leaving a freshly dug plot."

"Cody's not dumb!"

"Holly," Dad said, "there's another reason some murderers leave a trail to their doorsteps. Consciously or subconsciously, they know they've done wrong and they want to be caught."

"I still can't believe . . ."

"You did your best to help Cody," Dad said. "But now you've got to face facts, Holly. Give it up."

Bill lumbered into the kitchen, Frank and Mr. Ormond behind him. Bill held out a hand. Draped over it was a cloth that held some money, four credit cards, a woman's narrow gold bracelet, and two wristwatches. "We found this stuffed under Cody's mattress, near the foot of the bed."

Dad held out the knife and explained the switch.

"We've got more than enough to go on," Bill said.

"The money, the credit cards, the jewelry his parents were wearing—if Cody stole them, then why leave them here?" I demanded. "Why didn't he take them with him today?"

Frank groaned. "I can understand why he didn't. What if he were caught with them in his possession? He was afraid, wasn't he?"

Since Frank was looking at me, I answered. "Yes," I said. "He was terribly afraid."

One of the officers walked in from outside. He

held up a damp, badly wrinkled T-shirt. "This was in the washing machine out in the garage, along with a pair of jeans."

"Wrap them up," Dad said. "We'll send them to the crime lab."

Frank fell into a chair at the kitchen table and rested his head in his hands. "This is all so hard to believe," he said. "Cody's always been a good kid. He's not the type."

"There's no 'type,' Mr. Baker," Bill said. "As a rule, whenever somethin' like this happens, neighbors and relatives say, 'I can't believe it. He's always been such a nice boy.' What triggers the change from a 'nice boy' into a killer? Maybe anger that's built up over the years, or maybe an out-of-control temper that most people don't see. Sorry, but we don't have all the answers."

Another uniformed officer came into the kitchen and began to talk to Dad and Bill. As Mr. Ormond joined them, I said to Frank, "I don't believe, either, that Cody is the murderer."

Frank lifted his head. His eyes drooped with sorrow as he looked at me. "I didn't say I believed Cody didn't kill his parents. I did at first, but now there's so much evidence against him. Holly, I said it was *hard* to believe. That's all."

So many thoughts raced through my mind. I struggled to reconcile the inconsistencies.

Maybe I am stubborn. Maybe I'm just plain stupid, I told myself. But something here is all wrong. Why would Cody steal just a few pieces of jewelry and credit cards and then hide them? If he used the cards, he'd be caught. There'd be no point in taking them. And wouldn't he try to pawn the jewelry?

I could see the Garnetts' living room the way it had been when I visited it with Glenda. The answer had been coming toward me when I panicked and ran. Glenda had said we could try again. Did I have enough courage?

"Someone knows what happened in that room," I said aloud. *Maybe I can reach them. Maybe not,* I thought.

"Who are you talking about? You don't mean that old neighbor with all the stories to tell, do you?"

"Ronald Arlington? No," I answered.

Frank straightened, staring at me intently. "Who is this person, Holly? What do you know?"

The memories of the room flooded my mind, and I shivered at the blood and the fear and the terrible red glow. "It's at the house," I whispered. "I can't tell you now because I don't know if I can . . ."

Dad came up and rested a hand on my shoulder. "Go home, Holly," he said. "Sara's waiting to drive you."

Chapter Fourteen

As Sara pulled up in front of my house, I said, "I'm sorry I got you into that."

"It's okay," Sara said. "At that moment it seemed like the only thing to do."

"I thought I could help Cody, but I didn't."

"No one can help Cody but himself," Sara said. "At least now you can give it up, Holly. It's all over."

I shuddered. "That sounds so final."

Sara put a hand on my arm. "They'll catch him," she said, "and he'll go to trial. It will be awful for you to read about it and hear about it while it's going on, but remember—I'll be there with you. That's what best friends are for. Right?"

"Right," I said, "unless . . ." I tried to smile and couldn't quite make it, but I mumbled, "See you," and climbed out of the Jeep.

As I closed the front door behind me, I called out, "Mom, I'm home."

Mom called back, "I'm in the kitchen."

As I walked toward the kitchen, something on the coffee table caught my eye, and I stopped. Transfixed, I stared at the amber barrette! I'd hidden it so carefully.

"Mom!" I yelled, "where'd you find my barrette?"

I heard the click of Mom's heels as she walked from the kitchen. "What are you shouting about?" she asked.

"My barrette," I said and pointed to it.

"What about it?" Mom looked puzzled.

"I thought I . . . uh . . . lost it. Where did you find it?"

"It was sticking up behind one of the sofa cushions. Is that where you lost it?" She smiled. "Any other questions?"

My gaze was drawn back to the barrette. The red-gold of the amber lay still and cool and deep. Maybe its appearance was a sign, telling me what I should do.

"Well?" Mom asked.

"Could I borrow your car?" I asked. "I've got a couple of things to take care of."

"Like what?"

"Like . . ." I remembered two library books that were overdue. "Like the library, for one thing."

"If you're going to the library," Mom said, "there's a book you can pick up for me. They called and said it had come in. I'll write down the name for you."

Deliberately, I took my white barrette out of my hair, replacing it with the amber one. Under my fingertips the amber felt cold and hard.

I ran upstairs and picked up the library books just as the phone rang. I snatched it up on the first ring. Cody? But it was Sara's voice.

"Holly," she said, "what did you mean when you said, 'Unless'?"

"What are you talking about?"

"What you said when I took you home. We were talking about Cody and how it was over for him, and then you said, 'Unless'."

"So?"

"Don't play games with me, Holly," Sara said firmly. "What did that 'unless' mean? What have you got in mind?"

"Sara, you are my best friend. I only meant that I'm going to try one more time to prove that Cody isn't guilty."

"What are you going to do?"

"I promise I'll tell you if it happens," I said and hung up. The phone rang again, but I ignored it.

As I reached the kitchen, Mom handed me the phone. "It's Sara," she said.

"I've got to go out. Right this minute. I promised I'll call you later," I said to Sara. Without waiting for an answer, I hung up.

Mom had finished writing the book information on a piece of notepaper. "Thanks," she said and handed it to me along with her car keys. "When will you be back?"

"Soon," I said. "Six-thirty or seven. In time for dinner."

Wednesday. 5:00 P.M. It took less than five minutes to pick up Mom's book. I jumped back in the car and headed straight for West University.

I parked in front of the Garnetts' house. Then I ran across the street and up the winding path to Glenda Jordan's front door. I knocked, expecting the door to open at my touch, but no one answered. I knocked again, but the house was silent. I walked down the driveway and peered into Glenda's junglelike backyard, but it was empty. So was her one-car garage. Cautiously I reached up to touch the amber in my barrette. It was cold and lifeless.

Discouraged, I trudged back to Mom's car, but I stopped, my hand on the door handle. If I were going to make contact with the spirits in the Garnetts' house, it would have to be soon. Very soon. Tomorrow the cleaners would come to take up the rugs and scour the room. According to what Glenda had said, the atmosphere wouldn't be the same.

I had no choice but to try it alone. Before I could change my mind, I stalked up to the front door, unlocked it, and closed it firmly behind me.

Slowly I crossed the entry hall and entered the living room. The air in the house had been stirred by the presence of others, and I remembered that the police would have been here, searching for

Cody. "It's all right," I whispered aloud. "They've gone and I'm here. It's all right."

Trying to duplicate what Glenda had done in every way possible, I went to the entertainment center, found a tape, and popped it in.

I sat in the chair I'd been in before and carefully repeated what Glenda had instructed me to do. Palms resting upward in my lap, I closed my eyes and began thinking about my toes, willing them to relax. My thoughts moved upward: hips and back, shoulders, and arms, and, last, my neck and head. My breathing slowed. In and out, in and out, along with the music that grew in volume and swirled through my mind. I could sense the amber glowing as its warmth radiated through my body. It was time to seek the spirits. It was time.

"M-Mr. and Mrs. G-Garnett," I whispered, as I had before. "Here I am again—Holly Campbell. Cody's friend. Help me learn the identity of your murderer. Show me. Please . . . show me."

I pictured the room as I had before. In my mind I watched Cody place a CD in the player and turn to me, his arms outstretched. Then, as before, the music in my mind became harsh and discordant as the vision of Cody faded. I opened my eyes to a rush of hot red air that pressed against my back and head. The smell of evil was bitter and horrifying and wrapped itself around me.

At the edge of my consciousness I began to hear footsteps again. And as before, they slowly came closer . . . closer . . . closer.

Painfully clutching the arms of the chair, I

forced myself to be still and wait. *I won't run. I won't. I can't!* I silently screamed at myself.

A sudden stillness overpowered the room, and as I watched, unable now to look away from the door, the red haze parted. Out of the stillness and into the doorway stepped . . . Cody.

Chapter Fifteen

Holly?" Cody said, and the vision shattered. "You shouldn't have come here."

I was too shaken to answer. I remembered what he had said: *I want to be honest with you. There's something I have to tell you.* Sara had interrupted him, and he hadn't finished. Had he been going to confess to the crime? I'd believed in his innocence without question. I'd worked so hard to prove it. Was all my effort for nothing?

I was too numb and hurt and sick to be afraid of Cody. "The police were here, looking for you," I said.

"I know. I spotted the car. I waited, then drove into the garage after they'd left."

"How'd you get in without a key?"

"I got my keys back. Didn't I tell you?"

He walked over and sat in the chair Glenda had chosen. "It's funny," he said. "I thought I could run somewhere, just get away from everything. But there's nowhere to run. They'll be back here. The neighbors will watch for any sign that I'm around. And the lake house will be watched too." He leaned back and sighed. "There's nowhere to run, Holly. Nowhere at all."

"They found the murder weapon," I told him. "And the money and credit cards and the jewelry your parents were wearing."

Cody just shrugged. Then he closed his eyes for a moment, and his face sagged with exhaustion. "Oh, Holly, you don't know how much I wish I hadn't gone back. The first argument I'd had with Mom and Dad was bad enough, but then I came home again to get the keys and we were all so angry we were shouting at each other, and I threatened my parents. Why did I do it? I hate myself for it. Now, when I try to remember them, I can only think about the arguments."

"Wait a minute, Cody." Shocked, I suddenly realized exactly what he'd just said. I'd heard the words before, but they hadn't registered. "What can you tell me about the murder weapon and the things taken from your parents?"

He opened his eyes. "Nothing. I don't know anything about them."

"But your Uncle Frank does."

"You mean the police showed him?"

I wiggled to the edge of my chair. "Cody, where's your sleeping bag?"

"What?"

"Where is it?"

"I don't have one. I borrowed Frank's."

"Is it the same sleeping bag you brought back from your parents' lake house?"

"Yes. When I told Frank I was going to drive to the lake to pick up some clothes, he asked me to bring the bag back for him."

"So your uncle knew you were going."

"That's what I said."

"Cody!" I grabbed his arm. "Frank told the police—and us—that your parents had complained to him about your threats. If you threatened them when you came back for the keys, then Frank was at the house *after* you left the second time."

Cody struggled to take in what I'd said, and when it finally made sense, his eyes grew wide. "Frank was in the house after I left?" Cody shook his head. "No, Holly. You've got to be wrong. Frank couldn't have killed my parents. He's a nice guy. He's tried to help. He's taken good care of me."

"And he's been appointed as your guardian."

"Well, yeah. He'd pay the bills and sell the house and . . ." Cody broke off, groaned, and clapped his hands to his forehead.

"Frank made it look like *I* did it, Holly? Can that be true? Why?"

"Greed," I said. "He wanted the money."

"But won't he have to put most of it in trust or account for it to the courts?"

"If he's dishonest, he won't follow the rules."

"I don't get it. He could have killed me, too, but he didn't."

"If you were murdered with your parents, then Frank would have looked guilty. This way you'd go to prison, and he'd have the use of your money. Or maybe you'd run away. If the police saw you and chased you, you might even have been killed." I shivered at the thought. "Frank encouraged you to run, didn't he?"

Cody couldn't shake the horror. It twisted his face. "What will we do, Holly?" he asked. "Nobody will believe us."

"Dad will. We'll tell him. Your uncle won't get away with his plan."

"Yes I will. It was a good plan." Frank spoke to us from the doorway.

Cody started to rise, but Frank pointed a handgun at him. "Stay where you are, Cody."

Frank turned to me and said, "You should have done what Cody told you to do. You shouldn't have come here." He smiled. "Especially after telling me that whatever it was you were going to investigate had some connection with this house. All I had to do was come here to find you."

I was almost too frightened to breathe. My chest hurt so much it felt as if someone were standing on it. Frank had committed one murder, and I knew he'd kill us. Who'd be able to stop him?

The telephone was next to my elbow, but it was useless. I'd never be able to call 911 or Dad. Close to panic, I thought: *Oh, Dad, Dad! I wish you were here! I wish you could hear me!*

Someone can hear you.

As the words came into my head, I pictured Glenda. She had reached my mind before, hadn't she? Maybe she could again. With all my energy

189

and will, as Cody talked to his uncle, I tried to contact Glenda. *Help us, Glenda! We're in danger! Help us!* ran like an unending tape through my mind.

"You had a key I didn't know about," Cody said.

Frank nodded. "I knew about the extra key in the garage. Getting a duplicate made was easy."

Cody's eyes filled with tears. "How could you kill your own sister, Frank? How could you do any of this?"

Frank shrugged. "Holly told you. Money. I badly needed money. Your parents had it, and I didn't."

"You won't shoot us, Frank. You can't. There won't be any way to explain it."

Frank smiled again, as if he was having great fun with this game. "I won't have to explain it," he said. "The police will come and tell me all about it. Holly knew where you were going. You arranged to meet her here. She wanted you to give up, but you wouldn't. So you shot her, then killed yourself. Very touching. Very, very sad.

"Get up," Frank suddenly said, but before we could obey him, he waved the gun at us. "No. I changed my mind. Stay where you are. That's as good a place as any."

Glenda! Desperately my mind cried out, *Glenda! Send someone to help us!*

I heard a car screech to a stop outside the house. Another followed it. "Police! Open up!" a voice yelled. As the front door shook with hammered blows and the back door slammed open, I grabbed Cody and dived for the floor.

"I was about to call you, Detective Campbell." Frank's voice was smooth as Dad, Bill, and some backup police charged into the room. "I caught Cody and Holly here and planned to hold them until you arrived."

"No way!" I yelled as an officer hauled me to my feet and another one grabbed Cody.

"Dad!" I shouted. "Frank committed the murders and tried to make it look like Cody did it. And he was going to kill us!"

Frank shook his head sadly. "Poor Holly. She's so determined to prove that Cody's innocent, she'll say anything."

I forced myself to calm down. "Just listen, Dad. You told me you were fair, and you are. So just listen. Please!"

Frank smiled. "She's probably going to tell you some wild, unbelievable story," he said.

"I'm not going to tell you anything," I answered, thankful that I'd repeated every single one of Glenda's actions. Now it was my turn to smile. "I'm going to play a tape for you. Everything that was said in this room has been recorded."

After Frank had been taken downtown to homicide headquarters, Bill made arrangements with someone from Child Protective Services to take care of Cody.

Cody grimaced. "I'm not a child," he insisted.

"You're sixteen, son," Bill told him. "Legally, that means you'll get the supervision and care you need."

Dad told me to go home, but he let Cody walk to the door with me.

"Holly," Cody said, when we were out of Dad's hearing. "Remember, when we were at my uncle's house, I told you I had something to tell you?"

I nodded, and he said, "It's hard to say after all that happened and all that you did for me. I'll never forget it. Never! It's just that you and me . . . well, I mean, we've always been good friends, and I hope we always will be. I didn't want you to think you had to wait around for me if I was convicted and sent to prison. That would have made me feel terrible, because you deserve to have a life."

Still troubled, he went on, "And right now I guess I'm not ready for anything but trying to make sense of my own life."

I thought of how I'd wondered, for just an instant, if he had wanted to tell me he was guilty. I would never let him know what I'd thought. I would never let anyone know. I interrupted. "It's okay, Cody," I said. "I feel the same way. We're good friends, and for now that's all. Okay?"

I walked toward Mom's car with a sense of relief so huge it carried me along like a balloon.

I glanced at Glenda's house. The telepathy had worked. she'd sent for help, and I wanted to thank her for what she'd done. But as I started across the street, I saw Glenda's next-door neighbor, Mrs.

Marsh. She gestured toward the police cars. "Has there been more trouble?" she asked.

I skipped all but the most important news. "Cody's been proved innocent," I answered.

"I knew Cody was a nice boy," she said. As I reached the walkway to Glenda's house, Mrs. Marsh said, "If you're looking for Glenda, you won't find her at home. Her sister's ill, so she drove to Beaumont to take care of her."

"But I sent her a message. I thought . . ."

"She asked me to collect her mail. It'll be waiting for her when she gets back."

"Holly!" I heard Sara cry as she raced from Mrs. Marsh's house.

She hugged me, bursting out, "You're not hurt! I'm so glad!"

I hugged her back. "Sara! What are you doing here?"

"I knew where you were going! I knew what you'd do!" she said. "So I drove over here, I saw your car, and I knew you didn't belong in that house. Then I saw Cody's uncle drive up. He had something in his hand. I didn't know for sure what it was, but it looked like it could be a gun. I was so scared, it was hard to think. Glenda wasn't home so I banged on Mrs. Marsh's back door, and she let me use her phone to call your dad."

"It was *you* who saved us?" I hugged her again and burst out laughing.

"What's so funny? What happened in there?" She backed off and searched my face. "You're not having hysterics now that it's over, are you?"

"No, I'm fine." I stopped laughing and tried to explain. Remember when you said Glenda was using the power of suggestion with me? Maybe you were right, although I'm glad I didn't find it out until after I . . ."

"Make sense," Sara said. "What are you talking about?"

"Follow me home, Sara," I said, "and I'll keep my promise. I'll tell you all about it."

Mom had heard what happened, and her face was a mixture of happiness at seeing me and anxiety that I'd been in danger.

Sara had a million questions for me. Finally, as Sara was leaving, she winked at me and said, "You took care of Cody's problem. Can you get rid of your guilt about Paula now?"

"I hope so," I said.

"If I'd been the one who hadn't told on Mindy, you would have forgiven me, wouldn't you?"

"Of course!" I said.

"Then stop beating yourself with guilt. You ought to be able to forgive yourself as easily as you can forgive other people."

"Is anybody ever able to do that?"

Sara's smile stretched into a grin. "Probably not. But work on it, Holly. Okay?"

"Okay," I answered and grinned right back.

*   *   *

W*ednesday.* *10:00* P.M. When Dad arrived home, he found both Mom and me waiting for him.

"Jake . . . thanks for calling and telling me what happened," Mom said.

He smiled at Mom, but I had plenty of questions for him and couldn't wait.

"Cody was afraid of that woman who claimed she saw him in a convenience store. Where did she come from?"

Dad looked up, surprised. "There wasn't any such woman. That didn't happen."

"Then Frank made up the story!" Furious, I said, "He was trying to frighten Cody into running. Frank's a greedy, horrible monster!"

Mom put a hand over mine to calm me down. "You're the only one who really believed in Cody," she said. "I—we—don't approve of all the methods you used to try to help him, because even though they worked, you put yourself in danger."

"Both you and Dad said I was obsessed, and maybe for a while I was," I admitted. I wound my fingers through Mom's and smiled at her. "I used to be on your side. I got angry at Dad for neglecting us and spending so much time on his cases. But I understand now why he does."

I could see hurt in Mom's eyes, so I quickly added, "I'm still on your side, Mom, but I'm on Dad's side too. I found out he was right when he said after a crime takes place, everything happens fast. It *is* a matter of working nonstop to catch the truth before it disappears."

Then I grabbed Dad's hand, too, and held them

both tightly. "Maybe things between you can't go back to the way they used to be, but don't give up. I love you both so much, I'm asking, please, just try."

At first, Mom didn't answer, but Dad spoke up. "Lynn, all Holly asked was that we try," he said. "We can at least try. I know I will. I promise."

As Mom stared back at him, her gaze softened. "Yes, Jake," she said. "I do want to try."

I grinned at them both, so happy I could hardly stand it.

But there was one more thing left to do. I sat on my bed with a pen and a pad of notepaper on my lap. Glenda had tried in her own strange way to help, and she deserved to hear what had happened directly from me—but by mail, not in person. I felt easier at a safe distance from Glenda.

As I wrote, *Dear Glenda,* the phone rang, and I answered it.

Glenda's voice was soft as she said, "You are thinking of me, Holly, and I have been thinking of you."

A chill shivered up my backbone. "Y-Yes, I am thinking of you. I was just about to write and tell you about going to the Garnetts' house and what happened."

"I know what happened. You had the courage to seek the spirits and find the answer for which you were searching."

"Well . . . uh . . . sort of," I explained. "Except it wasn't spirits that gave me the answer. It was figuring things out and . . ."

She didn't give me a chance to finish. "Congratulations, amber girl," she said, and I heard a click as she hung up the phone.

As I got up from the bed, I wondered what I had been afraid of. *Forget all that stuff about clairvoyance and super powers,* I told myself. *Glenda's not magical. She probably heard about the arrest as soon as Mrs. Marsh could get to a phone, and then saw the story on the evening news.* Sara had been right about Glenda's power of suggestion. I refused to ever let Glenda influence me again.

I glanced at my reflection in the mirror over my chest of drawers and smiled. I was not an "amber girl." I was me—Holly Campbell—and I knew now that the spirit I had been seeking—and had found—was my own.

Joan Lowery Nixon has been called "the grande dame of young adult mysteries" and is the author of more than a hundred books for young readers, including *Shadowmaker*, *A Candidate for Murder*, *Whispers from the Dead*, and *Secret, Silent Screams*. She has served as regional vice president for the Southwest chapter of the Mystery Writers of America and is the only four-time winner of the Edgar Allan Poe Best Juvenile Mystery Award given by that society. She received the award for *The Kidnapping of Christina Lattimore*, *The Séance*, *The Name of the Game Was Murder*, and *The Other Side of Dark*, which was also a winner of the California Young Reader Medal.

Joan Lowery Nixon lives in Houston with her husband.